TROOPER TO THE
SOUTHERN CROSS

Also by Angela Thirkell in
A COMMON READER EDITION:

Tribute For Harriette

TROOPER TO THE SOUTHERN CROSS

ANGELA THIRKELL

"Leslie Parker"

THE AKADINE PRESS

Trooper to the Southern Cross

A COMMON READER EDITION published 2000 by The Akadine Press, Inc., by arrangement with The Thirkell Estate.

A COMMON READER EDITION and fountain colophon are trademarks of The Akadine Press, Inc.

ISBN 1-58579-022-2

25   10 9 8 7 6 5 4 3 2 1

1

How I got with the Diggers

I have always wanted to write the story of the old 'Rudolstadt' which took a shipload of Australian troops home after the War, but there were so many reasons against it. At the time we were all very angry, because it isn't a fair deal to put families on a troopship where there isn't any discipline, and we had plenty of indignation meetings and made plans for a great exposure of the whole thing, but somehow when Fremantle came in sight and we smelt the old smell of the bush right out at sea, we began to feel different. What happened at Fremantle was pretty bad all the same and nearly put the lid on it, and we had plenty of time to nurse our grievances again, going across the Bight. They wouldn't let us on shore at Adelaide because we had got such a bad name, and that made the diggers wild, though it was mostly their own fault. There was all sorts of talk about an armed guard to meet us at Melbourne and Sydney, but nothing was done, and all the bad eggs just went ashore and got demobilized quite peacefully. I expect some of them got their heads cracked in Melbourne when there was that rioting in the police strike, or at Sydney in the election rows. I have seen some pretty hard cases in my time – you don't see Egypt and Gallipoli and France with your drawing-room manners on – but these coots beat the band.

But when we really set foot on dear old Aussie again, we didn't much care what had happened on the voyage, and it is surprising how things that seemed important on a ship don't seem important on land. Also the other way round. When you are at sea all the little worries on shore don't seem to count at all. Before I left Sydney in 1914 I was worried to death because another fellow was chasing round after my girl, but the moment I got on the troopship all my worries seemed to drop off. Any worrying that had to be done was about other things.

We thought we were leaving Sydney to go straight to the War, but we had to go round by Hobart to pick up some of the Tasmanian lot. Coming round the west coast of Tassie we ran into really bad weather. Perhaps you know what the west coast is like. There is only one good harbour, Strahan, and that has a bar that will lift most ships out of the water. After that there's nothing till you get round to Burnie. Miles and miles of those cliffs they call organ-pipes, great rocks like pillars. If you get wrecked on them, you haven't a dog's chance. A hundred to one you are broken to pieces by the great south-western rollers that come booming up against the cliffs. If you have the hundredth lucky chance and do get ashore, you'll probably wish you hadn't. The bush is as thick as a bamboo clump, and there are great patches of horizontal scrub, a thing I never believed in till I saw it, and probably you won't believe in it either. It grows so close together that you can hardly force a way through, and then about twenty feet from the ground it sort of bends over and lies along in a sort of plaited roof. You can get along the top of it, but it is slow going, and if you fall through it is the dickens of a job to get up again. So what with mountains and gullies and nothing particular to eat and the thick bush where you can get lost within a hundred yards of your camp, the chances are all against you. That's why the escaped convicts used to eat each other – there wasn't anything else. Why, it's

2

only a matter of eighty miles or so from little Hobart to Port Davey, but very few men have ever been across that bit of country. My old grand-dad did it once, and when he had had one too many he'd talk about it for hours. Perhaps in a hundred years or so they'll have a road like the one by Lake St Clair to Queenstown, and petrol stations and cars going through all the time – perhaps they won't. Not if Labor goes on monkeying about with the government, anyway. Why, it would take about fifty years and fifty millions to build that road on a forty-hour week at the present rate of wages – and probably it will be a thirty-hour week by then if the Japanese haven't eaten us all. It seemed funny to me when I got to England and saw it all so neat and tidy to think of a little island only half the size being still unexplored. Well, explorers need something to do, and they would certainly get some kick out of little Tassie.

So this gives you some idea what kind of coast we were going along. Wind and rain all the time, water everywhere. The ship made twenty-three knots in twenty-four hours the second day out and most of the diggers were as sick as cats. We couldn't get much to eat either, because the cooks were as bad as the rest, and all the crockery was flying about, and the galley fires – the old 'Bendigo' was a small old-fashioned boat – were out. But the Major and I scrounged round and managed to get some tins of biscuits, and we put the fear of the Lord into one of the cooks and got some tea made. Gosh, those poor fellows were glad to get it. There was a great big fellow called Tiny Spargo, a bit of a lad he was and always ready for a scrap, and there he lay, looking green and grey and yellow and any colour you like to name.

'Brought the rum ration, Skipper?' said he with a kind of sickly grin.

'No,' said I, 'tea and biscuit, old man.'

3

'Christ!' said Tiny, 'but you've got to get something down if you want to bring it up, so let's have a go.'

I left him there and went to look at a man who had broken a rib falling down the companion way. I got a captain's rank from the jump, because I was with the Meds, and sometimes the diggers called me Skipper and sometimes Doc, but I answered to anything.

Well, anyway, I came back a bit later, after I'd strapped up the man, Les Holt it was, a stocky little fellow who stopped one in the early days of the Canal fighting, and there was old Tiny, still all green and grey and yellow, with an empty plate by him.

'Biscuit done you good?' I asked.

'My oath,' said Tiny, 'once down and once up, Doc.'

'Did you drink the tea?' said I.

'Have a heart, Doc,' said Tiny, looking greyer than ever, 'my stomach isn't too good. But it isn't wasted, I fed it to the ship's cat. Look, there's the old bastard as pleased as sin.'

And there was the cat having a nice drink of tea in the cup. The diggers loved that cat, and when we got to Port Said one of them pinched it, so that it would see life, but it got away and we never saw it again.

After three days we got round the west coast and the sun came out and the diggers got up on deck, and all was peace. They had a two-up school which of course was strictly against orders, but if the major chose to wink at it, it wasn't the doctor's business. And some of them had a game of housey-housey, and some of them sang very well, and they'd have singsongs going on half the day. So when we had collected a few more from Adelaide, we got away across the Bight. All this isn't actually part of my story, but it all goes to show what I was saying, that you forget your worries at sea quicker than anywhere.

You don't want to hear about the fighting on the

4

Canal, where the worst misfortune I had was when my horse put his foot into a hole on the Turkish side, and the hole was all full of a Johnny Turk who had been buried long enough to be pretty far gone. Talk of an escape of gas! All that Canal bit has been written about by real writers. Some of them were good on the job and some weren't. Mind, I haven't a word to say against newspaper men. We've all got to live somehow, and I've had some good pals among them, but some of these war correspondents fairly get me wild. I'm not going to mention names, because I don't know any law – the King's Regulations are all I know, and I know them backwards, and many a tight place they've got me out of – and I don't want to know any lawyers, and libel actions aren't any good to me, but any of you that were in Australia at the time the Prince of Wales came out will know what I mean.

So I'll leave all the War to correspondents, and missing out Gaba Tepe and the happy days in France, I will go on to the Armistice. There was one experience I had in France though that I'll never forget as long as I live. Somewhere round Pozières it was, and the diggers had had a good long spell of it, and when we got into a little village that wasn't quite in ruins they fairly pulled the place down to get something to eat. By the time I got there with my field ambulance there wasn't a crumb left in the place. I'd given my emergency rations to a kid we found yowling by the road, so I sent my batman – Ginger Kong his name was, half a Chink, but one of the best – to scrounge something for me. He was a good time gone, long enough for me to have a good long think about a nice thick beef steak with plenty of tomato or Worcestershire sauce, and scones with plenty of butter and jam, and a great big cup of tea, and I came nearer crying then than I ever have since I put my money on the wrong

5

horse for the Cup in nineteen twelve. Well, presently
back he came, looking as proud as you please. And what
do you think he'd found? A pot of pâté de foie gras and
half a bottle of Benedictine. I ask you! Well, I had to get
it down somehow. I didn't want to hurt poor old
Ginger's feelings, but it was a hell of a breakfast. I hope
I'll never go through an experience like that again as
long as I live.

Still you mustn't think I'm grousing. The War held
many a bright moment even for the diggers so far away
from good old Aussie. For instance, there was the day
the diggers got wild with the English A.P.M. and somehow lost him in the canal. I did my best with artificial
respiration, but the bugger had me beat. We had one
of the best laughs over that we'd had for many a long
day. The A.P.M.'s weren't any too popular with our
boys. They didn't seem to understand, and our boys are
pretty sensitive. If I wanted a job done I'd pick on a
good man and say: 'See here, old man, there's six or
seven of the boys lying on stretchers there, and they're
for it, I can tell you. Pass the word round to your cobbers
not to wake the poor chaps, and if any of you want a
bit of medical comforts, you know where to come.' Well,
they'd be as quiet as babies all night, and perhaps they'd
give the ambulance an extra clean up for me if my men
were dead beat, as they usually were, for they were great
workers. You need never have any difficulty with our
boys if you knew how to handle them. But the English
A.P.M.'s used to come blustering along, getting the boys'
backs up. The boys didn't like it, and they'd just say,
quite naturally: 'Aw, get along to hell, you bloody sod.'
Well, it was after that the A.P.M. got lost in the canal,
so you can't blame the diggers.

My people have a sheep station away up in the Western
District, not a big one, but enough to live on. Dad's

6

grandfather had taken up land sometime in the fifties, and he made a good thing out of it. Dad's father was a bit of a lad as far as I can make out – I don't remember him well because he died when I was just a kid. He wasn't tight that time; no he was just riding after some sheep quite peacefully, when his horse stumbled on one of those little volcanic rocks that stick out of those parts – they say all the Western District was volcanic way back in history – and grand-dad got his neck broken. It was a pity, because she was a good little mare, and after she'd broken her knees she wasn't ever quite the same. So then Dad carried on. Times weren't too good, and he has had to sell land now and again, but he still keeps going, though what with taxes and the shearers' wages and one thing and another, there isn't much to it.

My brothers took up some land further up country, and my sister married a mining engineer and goes all over the place with him, as they haven't any kiddies. But I never fancied the station life somehow. I dare say I got it from the Mater. She is partly English, her father was an English doctor who married one of the Mallards, fruit-growing people up in the Riverina, and though the Mater had never been to England, she seemed to have those kind of ideas. She was a great little woman, the Mater. I've seen her cooking for twenty shearers all the shearing season when she couldn't get help. And cooking means cooking with those fellows. A couple of sheep a day we'd kill then. The Mater would be up bright and early, getting tea for the men. Then there were chops for breakfast and plenty of tea. Then she would clean up a bit and put the joints in the ovens for dinner while she got them morning tea. We usually had the legs of mutton for dinner and the shoulders for tea, or sometimes the other way about, or sometimes she would cook the lot at once and have cold meat for tea, but the shearers would walk out on you as likely as not if they didn't get a hot tea. Then there would be afternoon tea for the men, and then for tea there would be a great spread with the mutton and plenty of potatoes and tomato sauce and lots of the Mater's scones and perhaps three or four big fruit pies or big jam tarts and the cheese and plenty of good strong tea. About nine o'clock we'd all have a cup of tea and be ready enough to turn in. Many's the time I've sat in the kitchen watching the Mater peel the potatoes, or heard her in the kitchen after we were all in bed, making scones or pastry for next day, thinking what a grand little woman she was. Dad thinks the same. He thought the world of her. Whatever time he came in, she'd always have a nice hot meal for him, and always shine his shoes if he was going into town to the store. Dad is one of the most hospitable men I know, and he'll never think it too late to bring a pal in for a drink or a yarn. When we were kiddies we used to have bets on what he would say when he came in, because it was always one of two things. 'What about a cup of tea and some of Mother's pie?' or 'What about cooking us a chop, old girl, and a nice cup of tea?' He's a great chap, the old man. I haven't seen him since 1911, because my grandfather – the Mater's father – left me a little money, and I decided to go to Sydney and do medicine, and then the War came, and somehow I've never been down to the old place since. The Mater died while the War was on. I daresay Jim and Arthur being killed had something to do with it. It was tough luck, but still Tom and Les are left, and Sis looks in from time to time, and Harry, the one that lost an arm, helps Dad on the station, so there's nothing to complain about. I manage pretty well in Sydney with my brass plate on the door, and though we haven't any kids we rub along all right.

The Mater used to write to some of her English relations. There was a Mrs French who was her cousin, and the two corresponded pretty regularly. This Mrs French was a widow and lived somewhere in London, and had a kiddy called Celia. So when I wrote to the Mater to say that I had joined the R.A.A.M.C. in Sydney and might be going to England any time, she told me to be sure to go and see Aunt Mary any time I was in London. I didn't see much sense in writing to Aunt Mary from Gallipoli, as I was more likely to be visiting the other side of Jordan than a widowed aunt in London, but when we got to France I did write. Aunt Mary wrote back a nice long letter full of news all about a lot of relations I'd never heard of, and said I must come and see them on my next leave. I must say one doesn't expect very much from aunts, but I thought Aunt Mary wasn't as enthusiastic as she might be about the brave nephew come to defend the old country and the rest of it. But anyway I forgot about it and lost Aunt Mary's letter with the address. Then I heard about the Mater's death and that shook me up a bit, and then my girl in Sydney wrote to say she was marrying Dick Parsons, who was on a newspaper and busy defending the Empire on the Australian front, so things were all pretty black.

I never thought Irene would let me down like that, but she did. I was pretty sore at the time, for I'd spent a lot of my pay on sending her presents and I'd even written a poem to her. It was lost with some of my kit in the big push before the Armistice, but it was a bit on the lines of some of the stuff in C. J. Dennis' 'Sentimental Bloke'. Funny, if you come to think of it, his girl being called Doreen and mine Irene. I did think of copying out one of his poems and putting Irene instead of Doreen, as they rhyme, but I was afraid Irene might spot it, as she

9

has quite a literary bent. However, it turned out to be the best day's work she ever did for me, so I don't bear her a grudge.

Well, naturally, things being so black, I spent my leaves in Paris and never thought of Auntie again. Paris is all right, but give me Sydney every time, or even Melbourne. Paris doesn't have the same homey feeling.

I had got my majority before the Armistice, and a friend I had at H.Q. put me wise about what to do next. He said some would be lucky enough to get sent home at once, but a lot would get stuck in England or France, and the best thing I could do was to apply under the Non-Military Employment Scheme. I went into it with him and it sounded a bonzer business. You got indefinite leave, on pay, to learn up your special subject, and our fellows were going for it bald-headed. Doctors, lawyers, architects, engineers, wool-mill owners, chemists, all sorts and kinds, it was the chance of their lives. They did say that old Colonel Rosenheim, the one that was one of the biggest crooks on the Randwick racecourse, got a job with some English bookies, but they couldn't teach him anything. But I can't say for certain. It was one of the best schemes the A.I.F. ever put up, and I was lucky to get in early on it. I had met one of your big English surgeons at a base hospital in France where we were short-handed, and we chummed up, and he told me to let him know if ever I wanted a job. So I wrote to him and he offered me a research job under him in his own hospital. It was my own special line of work, head operations mostly, and I jumped at it. So my pal at H.Q. wangled the thing for me, and there I was, on major's pay, and you know the Australian pay was a lot better than the English, doing the job of my heart with a man I liked. Luckily there were plenty of bad head wounds, so I was hard at it, learning every day and reading up the newest stuff most nights. I might go out with a pal now and again, but I stuck pretty close to work.

I had a pal in France, Eric Hudson, a fine surgeon, who was doing his N.M.E. (Non-Military Enjoyment the diggers were calling it now) in Paris, and he asked me to run down to the Plain some time and send him over a few things he had stored there with his kit. So one winter day I went down, and this is really where my story begins.

There was another old pal of mine down on the Plain, Jerry Fairchild, a colonel in the artillery he was. We had had some good old times together on the Peninsula, and we shall always remember gratefully that R.C. padre that gave us the whisky during the evacuation. Jerry had married an English girl just before the War. He is pretty well off and lives up north of Adelaide, but I hadn't met his missis, so I didn't blow in straight away, but I wrote him a line just to let him know I was about. He then asked me to come over to his place, so as I had a couple of days to spare, I borrowed a horse and rode along in the Colonel's direction. He had a little house somewhere over Amesbury way, so it wasn't a long ride from Tidworth. Jerry rode over to meet me, and we were going quite quietly along one of those country roads between hedges when two ladies came in sight. When we got up to them the Colonel said:

'Here, Tom, I want to introduce Mrs Fairchild to you.'

Then I got the shock of my life, because Mrs Fairchild gave one wifely look at her husband and walked right away from me. I wished the earth would swallow me. I didn't know what I'd done, but it was pretty plain that Mrs Fairchild had no use for me. Jerry didn't know what to do either, and the other lady just looked at us both and smiled, but didn't say anything at all. Finally

11

poor old Jerry dashed off after his wife, and I heard him trying to argue with her, but she just climbed over a gate into a field. His horse couldn't take the gate in that narrow road, so he had to ride along with his wife on the other side of the hedge, and they were arguing all the time. I had a little mare in France called Dinah who could have taken that gate. She was a wonder. Anything she couldn't jump over she would climb up. She was as cunning as a cartload of monkeys too. I taught her to do the Guards' salute with her tail. If we passed any of the Guards, the diggers would all turn out to see Dinah salute, and the Guards were as wild as anything. She was a great little mare, and I have often wondered what happened to her.

So there I was, all alone with a strange girl. She was a wonderfully pretty little thing.

'It's all right,' she said, 'it's not your fault, Major. It's just an argument that the Colonel and his wife have occasionally.'

'I thought something was wrong,' said I. 'Perhaps Mrs Jerry doesn't want to meet me.'

My horse was fidgeting all the time, trying to walk on all his own toes at once, the way they do, so I got off, and the girl said we'd walk along after them. When we got round the next corner, there were Jerry and his missis walking back towards us, both looking quite calm and pleased.

'See here, Tom,' said the Colonel, 'I want to introduce you to my wife.'

'That's better,' said the Colonel's wife, and she shook hands with me. She was a nice-looking woman, darkish and bright-eyed, and I could see at a glance who was master in that family.

'I'm pleased to meet you, Mrs Jerry,' said I.

'Well, now you must come back to a meal,' she said.

'I'm not sure if it's tea or dinner or supper, but Jerry will see that you get enough to drink.'

'I don't mind if I do,' said I.

Mrs Jerry turned round to the girl and said:

'That means Major Bowen thanks me very much and is delighted to accept.'

I didn't tumble to what she meant, but I supposed it was all right.

'Now, old lady, no more leg-pulling,' said the Colonel. 'We'll give Tom a nice homey evening and get some of the boys in,' and he reeled off a dozen names of men I knew.

It all sounded good-oh, so we walked along together, the Colonel and I leading our horses, and the girl began to talk to me and asked me if I had any friends in London. I said I had made a few, and I had an auntie there, but as I had forgotten to answer any of her letters I expected she couldn't be keen on seeing me. Besides, she lived out at Hampstead in the back-blocks.

The girl didn't know what back-blocks were, so I had to explain they were way out beyond everything. I asked her if she had read 'On Our Selection', because that gives you some idea of the back-blocks. But she hadn't. And she hadn't read 'We of the Never Never', nor 'While the Billy Boils', so I knew she wasn't literary. That made me like her from the jump, because I've not much time for that literary set, though mind you I've known some literary men who you'd never have known from anyone else. There was Joe Dickson who used to work for the 'Sydney Bulletin', you would just have taken him for one of the crowd. Last time I saw him he was going up Shrapnel Gully. Perhaps the Turks buried him – they were decent enough in that way; we didn't get the chance. He was a great chap, and I expect his one regret in passing out was that he couldn't send the story to his editor.

Anyway, the girl, as I said, wasn't much interested in literature, but she seemed quite annoyed at the idea of Hampstead being in the back-blocks.

'Why, I live there myself,' said she. 'Perhaps we'll meet.'

I wanted to say 'You bet your sweet life we will,' but I didn't know how she'd take it. So I only said:

'I'll go and see my auntie now, even if I didn't mean to before.'

'What is her name?' asked the girl.

'Mrs French.'

'But that's my mother,' she said. 'You are the cousin that wrote to her from France and then disappeared.'

And so I was. I could have kicked myself for not noticing her name when the old Colonel mentioned it, but I had got so tied up with the way the Colonel's wife had walked out on me that I must have heard the name without hearing it, if you know what I mean.

'Then you must be my cousin Celia,' I said, 'but I thought you were only a kiddy.'

So Celia laughed and said she was twenty-five, but I needn't let it worry me.

'Well, I'll believe it, but thousands wouldn't,' I said.

So we had a great old yarn about things. The Colonel and Mrs Jerry had gone on ahead, so I asked Celia to tell me right out what made Mrs Jerry so wild, but Celia said she couldn't explain, and I must ask Mrs Jerry myself.

The Colonel and his wife had two bonzer kids, Mary and Dick. Mary was seven and young Dick was five. I never knew a couple of kids I liked better. I daresay you have guessed already that I fell in love with Celia from the jump, so it's no use trying to make a mystery about

14

it, and when I saw Celia and the kids, and the way she was telling them stories and being just like a kid herself, I thought it would be fine to see her with kids of her own and mine. But we can't have everything we want.

Well, we all got very pally over our tea. A real dinkum Aussie tea it was: chops, potatoes, apple pie with cream, biscuits and cheese and celery, and the best tea I'd drunk for donkey's years – just like being back in Aussie it was. Presently Celia said to Mrs Jerry:

'My cousin Tom wants to know why you walked out on him like that, Frances.'

The old Colonel looked quite sheepish and tried to change the conversation, but Mrs Jerry was one of those women you can't stop. It seems she had kept some of her English ideas, and if the Colonel didn't toe the line about them, he got ticked off pretty quick. One of her ideas was about introducing people. You or I would say to a pal: 'Here, Joe (or whatever his name might happen to be), I want you to know the missis.' Or if you wanted to do it very correctly: 'I want to introduce Mrs Robinson to you' – that is if your name happened to be Robinson. But it seems this wasn't right according to Mrs Jerry's ideas, and she went right in off the deep end every time the Colonel opened his mouth. The idea was that you must introduce your pal to your wife and not your wife to your pal, though where the difference comes in you can search me. I don't see much in it myself, nor did the old Colonel. But ever since Mrs Jerry had left a garden party at Government House when he didn't do things the way she wanted, he had been pretty careful, and it was just a piece of bad luck that he got strafed about me.

Well, I was only down there for three days, but I spent most of them over at the Colonel's place, and when I went back to town I went up to Hampstead the first day

I could. The French's place was one of those old-time houses, a bit pokey, but nice and homey. I asked for Mrs French, and while I was waiting I had a good look round the room. I could see at a glance that Aunt Mary wasn't too well off. The room had that bare kind of look. The boards were painted and there was just a small rug in front of the fire. I would have liked to see a nice thick carpet right up to the walls, something your feet go right into. And there were only two easy chairs and a little sofa, and none of the furniture matched. I made up my mind then and there that if Celia would marry me I would make a real home for her. And so I have, and our little home in Sydney has one of the nicest suites of drawing-room furniture you ever saw. There is a nice suite for the dining-room, too, four chairs and two armchairs, all in leatherette, and a dining-room table and a bonzer sideboard all to match. There is quite an artistic window too in the dining-room, in the shape of a horseshoe, with a nice design in coloured glass. And the bedroom has a fine suite too, in Queensland maple with inlay. I always wanted Celia to have the best, and there isn't anyone who has a nicer little home up the North Shore.

Presently Aunt Mary came in, and she was quite nice to me, but a little stiff. I expect I had got across her when I didn't answer her letters. But I just sat down by her on the Chesterfield and had a good yarn about the family, and I told her about the Mater and what a great little woman she was, and she got much more friendly and asked me if I knew some people called Pember in New Zealand. She seemed quite surprised when I told her New Zealand was nearly a week's voyage from Sydney. As a matter of fact I have never been to New Zealand. They say it can be one of the worst passages in the world, though the people who say that can't ever have had a bad night in the Bass Straits. When you go across from Melbourne to Launceston you know what trouble really is. I'll never forget the time I went across in the old 'Loongana'. I was in a hurry to get over, because Irene – the girl that went back on me and married Dick Parsons – had gone over to stay with some relations, and I knew Dick was there too, and I didn't want him to get in ahead. It was all in the middle of the tourist season, and the unions were getting ready for their annual Christmas strike, so everyone was rushing to get across before the strike began. I couldn't get a berth in a cabin, but that didn't worry me, because I thought I'd doss down on deck. But that day a brickfielder began to blow. That's a north wind that comes from the interior and you'd say it came straight from hell. It's as hot as an oven and brings clouds of red dust with it, and the sun goes copper-coloured and sky goes lead-coloured, and all you can do is to get the washing in and shut all the doors and windows and hope none of your pals are out in Port Philip Bay, because if they are the first thing you'll hear about them is that their boat was found upside down and stove in. And it's the last thing you hear too.

By the time we had got through the Rip and had some tea, the old man ordered everyone below. I expect you've heard of the Rip. It's a kind of jumble of cross-currents that they keep at the entrance to Port Philip Bay, and if it doesn't knock your boat silly one way it knocks it silly another. Of course the big liners don't notice it so much, but on a boat like the 'Loongana', or the 'Oonah', or any of those interstate boats, many a passenger that would have stood the rest of the trip is knocked out in the first round. They arrange for you to get your tea before you get through the Rip, otherwise you wouldn't have a dog's chance. Well, I had a good tea, and then I

17

went along to the smoke-room and had two or three with some chaps I met there, and then I had to turn in because I wasn't feeling too good. The steward had found a berth for me in the big saloon. I've never seen another boat like that, and I hope I never will. It reminded me somehow of an old picture of the Death of Nelson that the Mater's people had up at Kurrum-bolong. It was a big low room with bunks all round it and some in the middle, and you can imagine what it was like with twenty or thirty fellows all being ill. I might have kept my end up if it hadn't been for the others. Anyway, I was soon right down to it, and I called to the steward to get me some brandy, but he wouldn't bring it unless I paid him first. I went right off the handle at that, and I got up and ticked him off properly. He was a pale chap with a little moustache and that nasty counter-jumper's manner that I can't stand. Funny thing, I had him under me as orderly for a spell in France afterwards, and by God I made him jump to it then. But he wasn't a bad chap when he had learnt to toe the line. I was quite sorry to see the last of him. Not that there was much to see, because the shell-hole was about ten feet deep, but you get a kind of feeling for the chaps that you have under you.

Next morning when we got into the Tamar the wind had gone down and I got up on deck. It was a bonzer morning with a mist on the banks and the sea all foggy, and the old 'Loongana' went up the river as peacefully as if we had never had that bucketing the night before. Presently a fellow came up to me and said:

'You're a pretty good sailor, aren't you?'

'Oh, I don't know,' I said.

'Well, you were quiet all right last night,' he said.

I had a good look at him and I saw he was the man

who was in the berth above me, and he had been as sick as a cat all night and had let the world know it.

'If you want to know how to be quiet,' I said, 'I can give you the dinkum oil on it. Hold your tongue.'

Then I went away, for I haven't any use for a man that can't keep his feelings to himself, especially when they are the sort of feelings that are going to upset everyone else. But I'll never forget that night in the old 'Loongana'. She went through the water like a crazy corkscrew. They say she came out from England under her own steam. I'm glad I wasn't on board.

As I was saying, Aunt Mary and I got quite pally, and then Celia came in and I knew my number was up. Aunt Mary asked me to come to the house as often as I liked, and that suited me O.K. I'm not much good at writing about love-making, so I'll miss out all that part, but anyway Celia and I were married not very long afterwards. I had got a new job at a big hospital up in Leeds, and Celia and I went up there directly after the wedding.

Horseferry Road Dragoons

I now come to the next part of my story, which leads on
to what I really want to write about. It was while we
were in Leeds that things began to get moving. Celia and
I weren't badly off, because I had my major's pay and
she had a little money of her own. We spent a few days
in the station hotel, and then we found some lodgings
just outside of town on the edge of the moors, not far
from the tram terminus. The landlady was a nice little
woman, but she didn't cook for us. She let Celia use the
kitchen whenever she liked though, and didn't make any
fuss about things. As for Celia, the poor kid didn't know
the first thing about cooking, but she soon got the hang
of it, and I can tell you it was good-oh to know there
would be a nice hot supper my little missis had cooked,
whatever time I got back from the hospital. Our hours
there were pretty regular, but there were a lot of our
chaps up and down the country on Non-Military Employment, and quite often one or two of them would blow
into the hospital to see me, and as soon as I'd finished
my work we'd go off somewhere and get a drink and get
yarning, and often I'd bring the chap home with me. I
often remembered the way we'd come along after a good
old yarn about happy days at Bullecourt or at Quinn's
Post, and find Celia waiting for us. It was great to walk
into our own little sitting-room and say: 'What about
some tea, babe?' and introduce her to my pal. Then she

would get the food out of the oven and make the tea, and we'd settle down to a real good talk. One thing that I appreciate very much about my little wife is that she doesn't pick on my old pals, the way some of these English girls the diggers married do. Nearly always she'd go off after tea and wash up the things, and then go off to bed, leaving us to smoke and yarn. Sometimes I'd take my boots off after supper and Celia would give them a shine for me, so that they'd be ready next morning. She was a great hand at polishing boots, as good as a batman, and it's a job I've never liked somehow. When I was in uniform she would turn me out as well as any batman I've ever had. Boots you could see your face in, spurs shining, all the brasswork as if a ship's company had been over it. She is a great little worker.

We have never had a quarrel yet. Sometimes we both get a bit nervy, but we'd always make it up before things got too far. The nearest we came to a quarrel in those days was about the tomato sauce. Of course at home the Mater used to make ours, dozens of bottles, and it lasted us right round the year. Many's the good meal I've had when I was a kid, chops, or sometimes a parrot pie if we boys had been shooting, and plenty of the Mater's tomato sauce. Of course we lived quite simply up on the station, and it wasn't till I grew up and went to Sydney that I found you oughtn't to put tomato sauce in the soup. But a few meals at the Australia, when I could afford it, soon showed me that for soup you should use Worcestershire sauce. I've not much use for this etiquette myself, but there are a few things it's useful to know. They don't seem to understand etiquette so much in England. I naturally like things nice about the house, so after we had been in our lodgings a few days, I asked Celia for the tomato sauce. You would have thought I was asking for the Bank of England, the way she took it.

21

She never seemed to have heard of it and said you only had it with veal cutlets. Of course I know things are a bit different in England; for instance the way you get your mustard mixed in the cafés. I know the cafés and the tea-shops in Sydney pretty well, and they always served their mustard just as it comes out of the tin. The other way seems to me extravagant and not half so tidy. But anyway, Celia got me a bottle of sauce, and we had chops one night and some nice fried steaks of fish the next night, and what with that and the bacon and eggs at breakfast, the bottle was finished. So we had to get some more. Celia soon got the hang of it, and she makes it herself now, and it's nearly as good as the Mater's. My Aunt Minnie at Pott's Point is a splendid worker, and she gave Celia some lovely bits of crochet work she had done. There was a cover for a tea cosy, and some doilies for cake, all beautifully crocheted, but the best of all was a white crochet cover for the tomato sauce bottle. You put the bottle in, and pulled it tight round the neck and tied it with a piece of ribbon, and it had the words 'Tomato Sauce' worked into the crochet. I must say Celia did appreciate it enormously, and she put it away for fear of getting it dirty. So Aunt Minnie worked her two or three more. They can be boiled with the laundry on Mondays, and just give that artistic touch to the table that I like. And Celia deserves it all. She is the best little pal a man could have.

One evening, after we had been there a couple of months, I got home and found Celia rather upset. I asked her what the matter was, and she showed me a telegram that had come for me. It was from Horseferry Road, to say we had been booked for a boat to go back to Australia the next week. Celia must have been crying over it all afternoon.

'All right, babe, don't get the wind up,' I said. 'We've

got to go some time, and you've got your old man to look after you.'

But the poor kid cried and cried. She said her mother would have fits if she went off suddenly like that.

'Well, damn the army,' I said. 'Some Horseferry Road blighters butting in as usual where they aren't wanted, I suppose. Cheer up, babe.'

When I began to figure it all out, I came to the conclusion we must wangle things somehow so as not to go. I know the King's Regulations on my head, and if this had been a proper army job I would have known just what strings to pull, but with Horseferry Road it was quite different. A lot of blasted N.C.O.'s who never saw France used to sit there giving cheek to officers. Oh, there's a lot to be said about Horseferry Road. In case you don't know about it, it was the Headquarters of the A.I.F. in London during the War. It was handy for the R.C. diggers, being almost next to the big cathedral at Westminster, and it was handy for anyone who wanted to shop at the Army and Navy Stores. Otherwise it wasn't much of a show. A kind of old building across a yard with a lot of sheds built on behind, and just crawling with N.C.O.'s and warrant officers. I never saw such a set of lousy counter-jumpers in my life. If you were a poor old digger who had been in Egypt, or Gallipoli, or France, they treated you like dirt, but if you had been sitting tight on the Plain, or a nice safe job behind the line, and had had a red band round your hat, you could get your pick of a job there. I never could stand that sort. But I am a bit of a diplomatist, and I never wasted time telling them what I thought of them, because they could do you a bad turn if they liked.

Figuring it out, I knew I ought to get another two months at the hospital, and then I'd be ready to move. I couldn't very well leave Leeds myself, so I said to Celia she'd better go up and see what she could do.

'Oh, Tom, I couldn't,' she said. 'They won't take any notice of me, and I'll only make a muddle of it.'

'That's all right, babe,' I said. 'You buzz off to London tomorrow and see what you can do. Perhaps you'll see General Levy, he's rather an old pal of mine, or General Legge. And you can stay the night with your mother. It will cheer the old lady up. What about something to eat?'

The long and the short of it was that Celia did go off to town next day. I can only go by what she told me afterwards. In case you are anxious, I may as well tell you at once that we didn't have to go by that boat, but as things turned out it might have been better if we had. However, it's all over now.

Well, Celia said she got to Horseferry Road all right – it's down a queer street full of barrows called Strutton Ground – and she got in easily enough and found the department that was dealing with repatriation. Then, by what I gather, she struck a snag, one of those damned warrant officers who get a pen behind their ears and sit in an office like little tin gods. Celia said she got nothing from him but a lot of damned insolence – just what a woman would get from those fellows. Horseferry Road Dragoons the diggers used to call them, and my word, they didn't like it. Just as the poor kid was going away in despair, who should blow into the room but General Legge. Leggy was a great fellow. He was one of our best surgeons and had a waiting list as long as your arm in Brisbane where he practised. I'd had a good deal to do with him on the Peninsula, and we always got on very well. Celia had met him when she was on the Plain with the Colonel and Mrs Jerry, and she had made rather a hit with him. He was a dear old fellow and did his work just as well when he had been lifting his elbow. Naturally

24

he wondered what Celia was doing up there. When she told him what had happened, he went right in off the deep end and fairly lifted the roof. That W.O. must have had the ticking-off of his life. I must say I've seldom known a man with such a command of language as Leggy. He was pretty good at most of them and could curse a Gippo, or a Johnny Turk, or a Boche in his own lingo, besides knowing every swear-word in the French language, and a few over. It must have been a treat to hear him tell off that W.O., and at the end he said he'd have him sent back to Aussie at once for interfering with one of his men. For he looked on all us army doctors as one big family and wouldn't allow anyone to come butting in, though mind you he would strafe us himself good and proper if we needed it.

I won't forget in a hurry that night near Villers Bret, when my field ambulance ran short of supplies and the wounded hadn't enough blankets. I had given my British warm and my tunic to two poor blighters who were half dead with wounds and exposure, and then I forgot myself and went to sleep. When I woke up I was half frozen and as stiff as a board, and there was old Leggy in among the casualties.

'Well, Mr Bowen,' he said in his sarcastic way, 'I suppose you think three corpses are better than two.'

I then saw that the poor fellows were dead. I had the wind up properly, because they oughtn't to have died without telling me, and I thought the General – Colonel he was then – would have me up on the carpet for letting them get away with it like that.

'I'm sorry, sir,' I said.

'Sorry's no good,' said the Colonel. 'Do you suppose I want you down with pneumonia? Have a drink,' he said, giving me his flask, 'and give me a hand with these other poor bastards.'

25

So I had a good pull, and then we got my coat and tunic off the dead diggers, and I was never so glad to get a coat on in my life. When we had got things a bit straight and the supplies had come up, the Colonel let fly at me. I've heard some pretty good swearing in my time, but the Colonel beat the band. I've always had a great respect and affection for the old chap since then.

When Leggy had quite finished with the W.O., he took Celia round and introduced her to the officer in charge of the shipping section, who arranged for all the transport of officers and their families. He was none other than old Larry Sievers, whose people lived up at Wanderagong near Mount Buffalo. I was up that way one summer, prospecting for a little gold. All that valley was turned upside down by the old-time prospectors. They used to get quite a bit of alluvial gold there in the old days, but it had petered out, and now it was all little farms. But if you liked to camp beside the Wanderagong creek and wash for gold, you might make enough to keep you in grub for a few weeks. I never got anything worth mentioning but I got to be friendly with the Sievers family and used to go round to their place of an evening. It was good-oh up there, right at the end of everything. Just where my camp was the track petered out, and there was nothing but a bridle path over the mountains to Omeo. Quiet – you would hardly believe how quiet it was. Except for the magpies and the rosellas and the parrots and maybe some kookaburras and the noise of the creek, you could have heard a pin drop. And in the morning the air felt as clean as – well, I can't describe it. You have to get away into the bush to know what I mean. When once you've felt the air there, nowhere else seems the same. It's great to think that for hundreds of miles you'll hardly find a township, and everything is as fresh as it was the day it was made. It's enough to drive a chap to poetry, if he was one of those writer chaps. But though I'm a fair hand at writing, having done English with honours for my leaving exam at school, I've never seemed to shape well at poetry, though I daresay with my experience I could do quite well if I had the time. I've read most of Banjo Patterson and Adam Lindsay Gordon, and I much appreciate Robert Service and some of Kipling.

Well, Leggy took my little missis and old Larry out to dinner and a show, and Larry told Celia to come to him next time and he'd see she got a good boat. So the poor kid came back as pleased as anything. So time went on till just after Christmas we got a fresh notification that we came next on the roster for Australia. I'd about finished up with my job, so we said goodbye to Leeds, where I think I've never seen so many ugly women in my life unless you can count the day I went to Sheffield, and came to Celia's mother for our last days in the old country.

First thing I did, I went down to Horseferry Road to see Larry.

'Well, old son,' I said, 'what have you got for us this time?'

Larry pitched me a long yarn.

'You can go on the "Rudolstadt", he said. 'she's a German liner and is only carrying troops below and officers and families first class. They say she was specially built for tropical voyages and the last word in comfort. If you don't fancy going in a trooper, there are a few cabins left in the "Ormolu" that the authorities have chartered for us, and I daresay I can get you in there.'

I didn't quite know. I didn't much fancy the 'Ormolu' myself. I thought it might mean a white shirt for dinner every night, and all that sissy stuff. I asked Larry, but he said all officers of the A.I.F. would be wearing uniform on the voyage. That disposed of one snag, but I thought I'd better see Celia first, so I told Larry I'd come back next day, and I asked him to dine with Celia and me and go to a show that night.

We had a nice dinner at the Oceanian Officers' Club and went out to some musical show. That club was a queer place. All the waitresses were real ladies, wearing uniform of course. Some were all right, nice quiet girls you could yarn to a bit while they served you, but some of them were pretty hot stuff. There was one little fairy, Marquise de something she called herself, but nowadays she would be called something different, and gold-digger would only be the beginning of it. Some of our fellows used to get pretty drunk there, but I was never in with that set. Beer or tea with my lunch perhaps, and maybe a port and lemonade with my dinner was good enough for me. I don't think you should drink much if you have a lady with you, and I must say when I got back to Australia I was pretty sick at the way I saw the girls drink in Melbourne and Sydney. Some would carry it and some couldn't, and I don't know which were the worst. Quite young girls too. When I got well into practice in Sydney I frightened one or two of them off it. Cirrhosis of the liver sounds a pretty tough proposition, especially if the girl doesn't know what it means. I like a cheery evening as much as anyone, but I have some very serious feelings about women, and I can say that no woman has ever seen me the worse for drink. As for Celia, her mother was a real old wowser and went clean off the handle if one so much as had a whiskey and soda after a long day's work. But Celia is a sensible little woman and sees that an occasional cocktail isn't going to break all the commandments.

We gave old Larry a cheery evening, and next day we blew into Horseferry Road. I had talked it all over with

Celia the night before. She had an idea she'd like to go by the 'Ormolu', because she knew some people that were going as far as Colombo, but I told her that she would like the 'Rudolstadt' much better. You see, I didn't know those 'Ormolu' pals of Celia's, but on the 'Rudolstadt' I thought I'd be bound to find some old pals and Celia could chum up with their wives. Well, that was where my toes turned in, but of course you can't tell beforehand how anything will turn out. Anyway, when I nutted it out with Celia, she quite agreed, so we decided on the 'Rudolstadt'. Larry had the map of the cabins spread out on his desk when we got there.

'See here,' he said, 'I can fix you and the missis up O.K. There's a cabin here you can share with Captain Knox and Lieutenant Smith just opposite the bathroom, and Mrs Bowen can go on the lower deck. There's an inside cabin where we've got a berth to spare.'

'Christ!' said I.

'Oh, the inside cabins are all right,' said he, 'they've got ventilators. And the two ladies that are there are real good sorts. One is old Puffy Williams's widow, and the other———'

'Oh, to hell with Puffy and all his widows,' said I. And I fairly hit the roof. I can tell you I made myself pretty plain. I told him I wasn't going to be separated from my missis on a troopship, nor at any other time, even if I had to go to General Monash himself about it. It wasn't the first time I'd taken something up to H.Q., I said, if anyone did the dirty on me like that. I didn't lose my temper, because I've found it never pays, but I talked to old Larry like a Dutch uncle for ten minutes. When I'd got a little of what I wanted to say off my mind, I laid off and let him have his turn.

'Kamerad,' said he. 'But just you look at the way we're fixed,' and he showed me the plan of the ship.

29

Well, that ought to have put me off from the jump, and I've called myself all sorts of a fool since, but as you will see I hadn't much choice. I never saw such a mess in my life. The 'Rudolstadt' was an ordinary liner, about 8,000 tons, with a couple of suites and a few cabins on deck. On the lower deck there were double-banked cabins down each side of the ship. The outside cabins had portholes, but the inside ones had nothing. Not like those Bibby cabins where you have a passage to your porthole and it comes in very handy for hanging clothes and stowing away your luggage. Some had a ventilator to the deck above that anyone could chuck the end of a fag or a bit of chewing gum down, and some had a ventilator to the alleyway. Some of these had been single-berth cabins and some had two berths. But the A.I.F. wanted to get on with the repatriation job, so all the single cabins were turned into two-berth, and the two-berth into three-berth. And all the two-berth cabins were on the inside, with no fresh air to speak of. I saw trouble ahead in the tropics, But I was too busy with my own troubles to let that worry me for the moment.

'You see how it is, Doc,' said Larry, quite ashamed, though it wasn't his fault, poor old beggar. 'The red tabs and the Adjutant have picked the deck cabins. We have two colonels going and they have the suites with their wives and kids. Most of the lower deck cabins are three-berth and how are we to fix up married couples? All we can do is to put the husbands together and the wives together. I daresay they'll make their own arrangements later,' said Larry, winking at me.

'My oath, they will,' said I. But just then Celia began to cry. The poor kiddie was quite upset about it. Poor old Larry got as red as a turkey cock, and I felt quite sorry for him. Then Celia let fly at Larry and told him she hated all Australians, and if she couldn't go with her husband she wouldn't go at all, and what did he think he was there for? I tried to calm her down, but then I got it in the neck, and she said she would go back to her mother and leave me to settle things, and if I couldn't fix up a decent cabin I could just get repatriated on my own. And then she banged the door and went off.

'Can you beat it?' said Larry. I can tell you I felt really sympathetic to the poor old blighter. It wasn't any good going after Celia, so Larry and I got yarning and we had a good laugh over old times on the Peninsula and the English R.E. colonel who always wore an eyeglass, even if he had nothing on but shorts, and then we got on to business.

'Well, Larry, what about it?' I said. 'Perhaps we'd better go on the "Ormolu".'

'No good barking up that tree,' said Larry. 'We filled her up this morning.'

'Then what do we do next?' said I.

'Search me,' said Larry.

So we had the plan out again and did some thinking. I saw one cabin that looked bigger than the others. It was on the lower deck, but it was a fair size and as big as two of the other cabins put together. As a matter of fact I found afterwards that there used to be a lot of cabins that size, but most of them had been divided into two, so that the ship would have more accommodation. The only other one that size was earmarked for the surgery. I showed it to Larry.

'That's for the Major,' said he. 'He wants it for himself and his missis.'

'I'm a major myself, if it comes to that,' I said.

'Yes, but he's on the staff,' said Larry, grinning.

'That's a fair cow,' I said. 'But never let it be said, Larry, that the Staff put one over on the Meds. Put him somewhere else.'

31

Well, after I'd talked to Larry for some time, I could see he was beginning to weaken. So we fixed it up that he would put the Staff major somewhere else, and I was to have the big cabin.

'And don't you make any mistake this time, you old bastard,' said I, for I was very fond of Larry. I haven't ever seen him again except once I'll tell about later. He got a job with a shipping firm in London and stayed on in England, and I believe he is doing very well. So we arranged to go to a show again the next evening, and I went off to Hampstead. I could hardly get out of Larry's room for the crowd. There must have been about twenty people waiting to fix up about boats by that time. But that was just like Larry. He never made you feel he was in a hurry.

I must say I got the wind up a bit when I got back to Hampstead, wondering if Celia was still mad with me. But as I came out of the Tube station, there she was, come to meet me. The poor kid thought she had upset me, and I might have gone straight off to Australia without her, or some kind of nonsense. She hadn't been home because she didn't want her mother to see she had been crying, so as far as I can make out she had been sitting in a tea-shop opposite the Tube station on the chance of catching me as I came out and making it up. Of course I was as pleased as anything at having her come to meet me, and I never said another word to her about the way she had flown out at me and Larry. I always have a very protective feeling about women. They are different from men somehow, and if we took notice of them everytime they went off the handle, life wouldn't be long enough for it. She tried to explain about it, but I shut her up very kindly and said we wouldn't talk about it again.

We now had the business of packing to undertake. It was easy enough for me, as most of my kit had gone west one way or another. The diggers were a wonder at borrowing things. A lot of my stuff got borrowed, as I mentioned before, in the offensive before the Armistice. I got a few things back, but I lost my diary and a lot of letters and a spare revolver that I was very fond of and some Boche souvenirs and a lot of equipment. I had some kit stored on the Plain too, and I must say I felt a bit sore when I found that had been gone through too. Somehow you didn't mind the diggers borrowing things in France. After all the poor chaps were having a pretty hard time. But to think of those blighted N.C.O.'s down at Tidworth pinching stuff off men who were fighting made me wild. However, it's no use whining, and I decided I'd do with as little as I could and wait till I got back to Australia to buy civvy clothes and things. For one thing I like travelling light, and for another I mostly wore uniform, unless I was in hospital, so it didn't seem worth while buying London clothes that would make me look all dolled up. Some of our fellows went to the smart London tailors like Moss Bros., but Sydney is good enough for me. David Jones in Sydney, or Myers in Melbourne always suited me to a T, and I didn't see the sense of standing up and having a tailor crawl all over me with his survey tape when I could walk into a neat ready-made suit.

It is a funny thing though the way some of your English tailors get their coats all smooth across the shoulders – or else it's the English men have a different kind of figure and not so well developed. You will always notice that an Australian's jacket comes up in a wrinkle across the back of his neck almost from the jump. I must admit I never noticed this myself till Celia told me, but once it had struck me I couldn't help seeing it. But it isn't the coat that matters really, it's the man who wears it. When I said to Celia that if I wasn't good enough for her in a coat of Australian wool, grown here and made by Australian tailors, I wouldn't be good enough in a robe and halo, she only laughed. But I must say now I have noticed it I do sometimes wish my coats didn't wrinkle across the back the way they do.

But Celia's packing was another question, because she had some bits of furniture of her own she wanted to take out. I didn't see the sense, for we could get just as nice things in Sydney, but the kiddie was set on it. There was a kind of medieval table and a bureau and some rugs and a grandfather clock and some pictures. And what must the poor kid do but bring her old cradle. A funny sort of affair it was, made of wood and cane, for all the world like some of the kitchen chairs at home. I expect she hoped – but oh, well, it's no use talking about it, and when we found things seemed a bit hopeless I got some nice ferns and pot plants and put them in it, and it is quite a feature of our little drawing room. It's not that I don't feel things, because I am wonderfully sensitive, and I'd love to have had a whole crowd of kiddies, but you must make the best of things in this world and the pot plants do look bonzer. And she had an idea too that there were no comfortable beds in Australia and wanted to bring her own. That was all very well, but a bed takes up a lot of room to pack. Besides I am old-fashioned enough to feel that a wife's right place is beside her husband.

So before I knew what was happening, there were four big packing-cases and two or three smaller ones. One of the pictures was a strange kind of affair, but somehow it had a great attraction for me. I have always had a great appreciation of art and thoroughly enjoyed the land-scapes of Arthur Streeton and Hans Heysen. As for

Norman Lindsay, some of the fellows at the University used to collect his pictures, but I have a certain feeling of reverence for women which prevented me buying any, though I am broadminded enough to enjoy looking at another chap's collection. The worst of collecting Mr Lindsay's pictures is that it is such a trouble to have a lot of drawings that you have to keep put away for fear the girl or the lady help might give notice. Some of the fellows who collected them used to keep them in a box under the bed which they said was the best place for them, but there is such a thing as carrying a joke too far. I have a pretty keen sense of humour myself, but a thing must be really funny to get my appreciation.

Well, this picture of Celia's was a sketch of a woman in an old-time kind of gown, something in the crinoline style, sitting all hunched up with a lot of things strewn about her and a kind of little flying fox up in the air holding a label to tell you the name of the picture. But being an antique, the spelling was the old-fashioned one of Melencolia. In spite of this, and of the fact that the artist was a German, which may also account for the spelling, that picture always got me thinking. It was the occasion of quite a scene at Sydney, as you shall hear later. Unfortunately I never seemed to have time to see the picture galleries in Paris or London, but I know I would have appreciated them very deeply.

The question now was: how much luggage could we take with us? Celia had got a paper about luggage from Horseferry Road, saying exactly how many cubic feet were allowed for each passenger. I've forgotten how many it was, but though it looked a lot on paper, as cubic contents always do, it boiled down to about one cabin-trunk and one suitcase in the end. Celia had gone to a Transport Agency to enquire about having our big cases sent out by a cargo boat, but what they wanted to charge would have left us broke for the next two years, beside not knowing how long it would be before we got them. Celia was getting quite nervy about it, so I said we'd go down to Horseferry Road and see what could be done.

The first man I ran into there was Jock Maclaren, a stocky little fellow from Turramurra. He had been promoted from sergeant to commissioned rank in France, and was a second lieutenant in the artillery. I saved his leg for him after Villers Bret.

'Well, Jock,' I said, 'how are the guns?'

'Listen, Mr Bowen,' he said, 'I'm not with the guns now. I used to be in the shipping office in Sydney, so they've put me here on the shipping. Anything you want sending to Sydney you just let me know.'

'You're the man I want,' I said. 'This is Mrs Bowen, and we've a lot of stuff to take out with us, and those sharks in the passenger department won't let us take more than a suitcase. What can you do?'

Well, we went and had morning tea in a café in Victoria Street, a mean little place compared with the Sydney cafés, down a flight of steps in the basement. Jock said no one was taking any notice of the regulations. One of the diggers, a lance-corporal in the infantry who owned a big station up in Queensland, was taking a grand piano and a special bath with fittings that had taken his fancy at some show, and another was taking a whole drawing-room suite. So if we didn't take our stuff too, he said we'd be mugs.

'I'll tell you what, Mr Bowen,' he said. 'Tell me where your stuff is and I'll send over a lorry and a couple of boys and get it all down to the ship for you, and it's no trouble at all.'

He was as good as his word, too. Next day a lorry came along to the place where Celia's things were stored, with two great beefy fellows in charge, and they loaded her things on and drove away. And the next time we saw those cases was the day after we landed in Sydney.

I have always been lucky with my pals and usually find someone to give me a hand. It's one great advantage of being a doctor that people seem to do you good turns. The way poor old Jock spoke about his leg, you'd think I was the only doctor that had ever put a leg in splints. There is no one more warm-hearted than the digger, and he'll remember any little kindness and never be happy till he gets one back on you. There was little Moses Colquhoun – at least his name was really Vernon, not Moses, but his father was Ben Cohen all right, so we used to call him Moses for short – that was hurt in the first landing at Gaba Tepe. The old 'Colne' was being used as a temporary hospital and, God, she stank. Our boys were wonderful, just keeping their spirits up and never letting out a sound, with the warm, sickly smell of blood everywhere and the Turk blazing away from the fort and the British Navy blazing back. I was doing what I could till we could get the poor blighters off to the real hospital ship. Little Moses was brought on by a couple of men. He had been severely peppered on the seats of his pants while getting over the gunwale of a boat with a landing party, and thought he was going to die. I hadn't any time to waste in sympathy, with lots of other men waiting with stomach wounds, but I bandaged him up and gave him a cigarette and put my coat over him for it was a cool night, and went on to the others. Would you believe it, from that day I was little Moses' white-headed boy. Old Papa and Mamma Cohen sent me comforts all the while I was in France and when later I set up my practice in Sydney, Moses sent all the Colquhouns and Cohens along to give me a start. Celia took

37

a great fancy to him. There used to be a lot of joking about the Jews, but we had a lot of real white men in the A.I.F., and if one or two of the higher ones had a bit of a reputation for using the digger to their own advantage, well, none of us is perfect.

3

Larry gives us the Dinkum Oil

Our boat, this old 'Rudolstadt', was to leave Devonport early on a Friday. Not that I attached any importance to superstition, though many do. When we got the notice about the boat train, it was a bit of a shock, for it left Paddington at 6.30 a.m. Not a nice time to leave London on a January morning. Of course Aunt Mary got the wind up and said we'd never wake in time, and were we sure the alarm clock was working, and should she get the telephone operator to ring us up and so on. But Celia was wonderfully patient with her mother and told her to leave everything to me; which, if you come to look at it, was the wisest thing she could do, as it was Celia and I that were going to catch the train, and not the old lady.

I hired a car from a garage near by, as we had rather a lot of luggage, and I took Celia and Aunt Mary to a show and supper the night before, just to cheer them up, and by the time I had done my own packing it was time to be starting.

It was pitch dark of course and a cold, raw morning, but Aunt Mary's help was a nice girl and she was up bright and early and had got us a nice hot breakfast. I always make a point of being friendly to the help, because they will do many a little thing for you which they otherwise would not have done, and I always think that a hot breakfast makes a lot of difference. Aunt Mary wanted to come to the station with us, but I knew Celia

39

didn't want her to come, so I persuaded her to stay at home. Her niece was coming to stay with her for a bit, so she wouldn't be lonely. I got very fond of Aunt Mary. She was a kind old soul and reminded me a bit of the Mater's sister, the one that was a bank manager's wife in Geelong. She died about two years later and Celia was much cut up about it.

When we got to Paddington, you would have thought the whole A.I.F. was there. It was like the days when the men were going back to France, except that everyone had piles of luggage and no rifles. I must hand it to the English porters for the way the heavy luggage had been put on the train. All the big trunks and cases were stowed away in alphabetical order in the luggage vans, so I could see we would have no trouble in finding our things once we got on board. There were wives and kiddies all over the place, relations saying good-bye, women crying, porters shoving trucks about, children getting lost and found again. Only officers' wives were going on this trip, so the diggers' wives were saying good-bye for the present and coming out later to join them. Lots of the diggers sent their wives first-class passage money later. Others just faded away.

Although we were half an hour too early, the train seemed to be crowded already and some of the diggers had stormed a first-class coach and were cheering out of the corridor windows. God, they deserved to go first class if anyone ever did, but after all there were officers' wives to be considered, and it isn't like our men to show discourtesy to ladies. I thought they looked a fairly tough crowd, but I didn't pay too much attention, as I wanted to find seats for me and Celia. We walked along the platform, looking into every carriage, but they were all full. Suddenly a well-known face came out of a window. Who should it be but the old Colonel.

'Come in, Tom,' said the Colonel, 'we've squared the guard and got him to lock us in here by ourselves.'

The guard came up and let us in and locked the door again, much to the disappointment of about a dozen men who hoped to get in. There was old Jerry and Mrs Jerry and Mary and young Dick and a girl they had to look after the kiddies. Gladys Barnes her name was, but she will keep. I can tell you I was glad to see Jerry, and I was glad Celia would have Mrs Jerry and the kids to talk to. She was looking a bit white poor kid. Mrs Jerry fussed round her a bit and of course blamed me as if I was responsible for the boat train starting at that early hour.

'Have a heart, Mrs Jerry,' I said. 'Think you are changing at Albury on the way down to Melbourne, and it won't seem so bad.'

'You are a Job's comforter,' said Mrs Jerry, quite snappish. 'To think of going back to a country with three or four different gauges, so that they have to turn you out of your train in the middle of the night.'

The Colonel tried to make things better by saying anyway there was only the one gauge between Melbourne and Adelaide.

'Yes, and even then they can't give you a dining-car, and turn you out at Serviceton to scramble for your breakfast with a crowd of nasty unshaved men. One thing, though,' said Mrs Jerry, looking round for all the world as if she were daring me to contradict her, 'is that it will make it harder for the Japanese.'

'Well,' I said, as no one was saying anything, 'I'll be the mug. Why the Japanese, Mrs Jerry?'

'Because, Major Bowen, when the Japanese invade Australia, which they will do when they've finished wiping their boots on China, they'll have no difficulty in landing wherever they like – especially if they choose

41

Cup Day with all the battleships bottled up in Port Philip Bay. But whatever railhead they capture it won't do them much good, because they'll have to spend all their time changing. By the time they've got, say, from Perth to Melbourne, they'll wish they'd never started, or the Trans-Continental had never been built.'

'But suppose they land at Melbourne,' I said. And there was something in what she said about Cup Day, because it has always been a standing joke how the fleet managed to blow into Melbourne just about Cup time. One year the admiral got so wild at all the jokes that next time he wouldn't let them come. But this was not popular.

'All you'll have to do in New South Wales is to destroy your rolling stock,' said Mrs Jerry. 'It will take them the next two years to build rolling stock for your narrow gauges.'

I didn't think this a sensible remark. It is just like a woman to say a thing like that. To begin with we wouldn't want to destroy our rolling stock, and even if we did, who could prevent the Japs sailing round the coast and coming right up the harbour? So I said so. Mrs Jerry said perhaps I was right. She was really a very sensible little woman, but got rattled at times.

Soon after this the train started. The boys were all singing and cheering and waving out of the windows. Mary and young Dick were waving too. I must say I felt a bit sentimental myself to think I was starting back to good old Aussie with my little missis.

It was a long journey to Devonport. Our train stopped pretty often in sidings, to let other trains go by, and every time some of the diggers would get out. I heard afterwards that three or four men had borrowed some money off their cobbers and not got back on to the train. I don't know what happened to them. We had all bought sandwiches, and we had a big flask of tea and the kiddies had chocolate and bananas. Presently the kiddies got sleepy.

'Go outside and have a smoke, you two,' said Mrs Jerry, 'while I get these children to sleep and have a talk with Celia.'

So the old Colonel and I went out into the corridor and had a smoke and a yarn. I said I was surprised to see him on the train, and he told me that they had to put off going on an earlier boat because young Dick had measles. Then he said let's go prospecting a bit.

'That'll do me fine,' I said.

So we went along the corridor, through five or six coaches, mostly full of diggers. When they saw us they started singing 'Have you seen the Colonel?' and 'Have you seen the Major?' A good song, but not the sort for a drawing-room.

'All right, boys,' said Jerry to one digger who seemed a bit above himself, 'wait till you're on board, and it will be "Have you seen the steward?" '

Well, the digger has a wonderful sense of humour, and in a minute the whole carriage-full was singing it – with illustrations. They were a cheery lot. Jerry and I went back to our own compartment. On the way we ran into a Staff colonel who Jerry knew. He introduced us. It was Colonel Picking. I had known his brother on the Peninsula – one of those blighters that give the men all the dirty work and keep their own hands as clean as they can. As a matter of fact he was such a nuisance that when he got a bullet through his arm I got him sent back to hospital in Egypt and passed the word that we never wanted to see him again. It was just as well the Turks did it, or the diggers would have put a bullet through him somewhere else. He got an adjutancy after that, which was about all he was fit for. I have never had much use for adjutants. The diggers used to call him old P. and S. – at least they used another adjective than old – which was short for Picking and Stealing. Jerry and Colonel Picking had a bit of a yarn and then we moved on. The diggers were still singing, and I had an idea there was some beer about. Jerry stopped me before we got to our compartment.

'See here, Tom,' he said, 'this is serious. Picking is in command of this boat.'

'Well, thank God it isn't his brother,' I said.

'You'll be praying that it was before long,' Jerry said. 'Of all the incompetent old foozling rotten-gutted . . .' well, he went on like that for quite a time, but not so that you could repeat it. It seems Jerry had been on a job with him in France, and anything this Picking could do without being actually cashiered, said Jerry, he did. It wasn't so much that he had any actual vice in him, as that he hadn't anything at all. He was just one of those born scrimshankers that get boosted up the army because they take good care to keep in with H.Q. I must say all this didn't sound any too good. If the O.C. troops is all right, everything is right. If he isn't, God help the poor digger. However, it's no use meeting trouble halfway.

It seemed hours before we got to Devonport. The train drew up just outside the station and we waited there for ages. When we did get up to the platform it was bitterly cold and raining a bit. Our little party all stuck together and followed the crowd, and got on to a sort of platform where there was a gangway to a steamer. Of course the kiddies began to jump and shout: 'That's our boat, Mummy.' Mrs Jerry took one look at it and she fairly jumped on the old Colonel.

'Why on earth didn't you tell me we had to go out in a tender?' she said. 'We shall be drenched and the children will get colds. Oh, how like you.'

44

The old Colonel showed great tact, I thought. He said: 'Well, old girl, it's an English port and an English ship. Don't blame it on me.'

Somehow we got on to the tender and I found a fairly sheltered place for the Fairchilds and Celia, while I went round to prospect a bit. Luckily it had stopped raining by this time, though everything was damp and beastly. I found a fellow I knew in the infantry, Jack Howe, one of the best, and he had his wife with him, a pretty dark girl. She was English too. Presently she said:

'If you want to see the last of old England, Major, come and look at the luggage.'

They took me along to where the luggage was being put on board. Well, I saw the bad quarter of Cairo after the diggers had been through it, but it was nothing to the mess on deck. I've worked a bit in mines and out on the back-blocks to earn money in my University vacations, and I've met some pretty tough cases, especially among the miners, but I can honestly hand it to the English stevedores and porters that were lumping our kit on the tender. All that stuff that had been packed in so neatly at Paddington was being torn out and chucked on board anyhow. Those fellows seemed to be taking pleasure in doing all the damage they could. If one or two of them were handling a good strong packing-case with iron bands round it, they just seemed to take a pride in chucking it on the top of a pile of trunks. I saw one great wharf-lumper pitch a great wooden case right onto a cabin trunk, so that the corner stuck right into it. The alphabetical order had all gone by the board by then. You'd have thought they were the salvage corps throwing things out of windows to save them from being burnt. If they'd had axes they'd have used them too. I reckoned at this rate we could count ourselves lucky if we ever saw our stuff again. Here my sense of humour got the better

45

of me, as I had to go and fetch Mrs Jerry, to show her what the English were doing. I wished afterwards I hadn't, because when she saw one of her trunks being pitched down on deck and the end bursting open, she fairly hit the roof. She blamed it on me, and she blamed it on the old Colonel, who had come up, and she blamed it on the whole A.I.F.

'Have a heart, Mrs Jerry,' I said. 'It'll be all right when once we get on board, and you'll find our men will look after you all right.'

But she gave me a sour kind of look and walked off. The old Colonel stayed behind.

'I've heard something, Tom,' he said.

'Pass it on, Jerry,' I said.

Well, he told me one of the sailors on this tender told him they had taken on a load of prisoners on board the day before.

'Well, they've got a guard, I suppose,' I said.

But the Colonel said he didn't like it. And he liked it much less as time went on, and indeed so did we all, as you shall hear.

By this time they had done all the damage they could to the luggage, so we got under way. One or two of the diggers had been having a scrap with some of the railway porters and got pushed into the water just then, but we easily fished them out and all their friends who had flasks gave them a drink. Up came a padre, one of those little men you wouldn't know again if you saw him, if it wasn't for his dog-collar. It is strange; our fellows have a wonderful amount of tact and common sense as a rule, but put them in a dog-collar and they will act just like other padres. This little fellow, Dart his name was, seemed to be just like the rest, though I daresay as a bank manager he'd have seemed quite a decent chap.

The moment he saw those poor fellows getting a drink he went off the handle.

'I must protest, Major,' he said, 'against our brave fellows using stimulants on every occasion.'

'Well, Padre,' I said, 'you chuck the bottle in the sea and the diggers will chuck you in, and then you'll both get pneumonia and we'll give you a nice cup of cocoa.'

I oughtn't perhaps to have said this, but I am well known for my quiet sarcastic way and I couldn't help taking this opening. Besides which, I didn't want to start in with a pneumonia case on my hands in the Bay. Some of the diggers had heard me, and they passed a few remarks about Dart.

'Well, let me tell you men,' he said, all red and flustered, 'this is a dry ship, and the sooner you learn to do without that poison the better.'

The men, who were a tough looking lot, began to laugh.

'My oath, it's dry,' one said. 'Seen the parson's case of medical comforts go aboard?'

Of course this made Dart angrier than ever and then something was said about communion wine that got him fairly wild. I do hate padres – always with exceptions of course and you will hear of one later – but I couldn't have the poor little runt made fun of in public. After all he held officer's rank. So I said a few kind words to the diggers and they melted away. Then I said a few kind words to Dart, and told him that if those fellows that were wet got pneumonia and died, he would have to answer for it if he stopped them getting a drink. So having made everybody happy and comfortable I returned to my party. The tender was rolling a bit and Mrs Jerry didn't look too good. Luckily Celia is a splendid sailor and she and the kiddies were all right. Just before we got

47

to the 'Rudolstadt', which was lying some way out, the nurse, Gladys Barnes, came up to Mrs. Jerry.

'Could I speak to you, Mrs Fairchild?' she said.

'It's no good giving notice,' said Mrs Jerry, all weak and green, 'unless you want to swim back.'

'Oh, it's not that, Mrs Fairchild,' said the nurse, 'but I want to ask you and the Colonel to call me Gladys instead of Nurse. Some of those common soldiers heard you call me Nurse, and they have been extremely rude and impertinent, calling out to me to come and put them to bed and tuck them up.'

The Colonel and I looked at each other, for the nurse was one of those very refined prim young women that give you the faceache.

'Leave Mrs Fairchild alone,' said the Colonel. 'You can be called Mary Pickford if you like, but wait till we've got off this damned Luna Park business.'

Luna Park, I will explain for such as do not know Melbourne, is an entertainment park where you go on switchbacks and slide down chutes sitting on a mat, and visit the Home of Horrors, etc. I imagine the old Colonel was thinking of the kind of sideshow where you sit in a boat and get bumped about by electricity, which never appealed to me.

Well, we now got to the 'Rudolstadt'. A lot of diggers were already on board and were chiacking their cobbers on the tender. Luckily I've been about a good deal on the interstate boats, and on the P. & O. and Orient liners before those government fools started tightening up the shipping laws and preventing you travelling except by interstate boat, and I know my way about a ship. I got Celia and her cases up the ladder and on to the deck before the others had begun to get a move on. Looking down on the tender I saw there was trouble ahead. There were two ladders, one for officers and families and one

48

for diggers, but there didn't seem to be anyone there to keep order, and the diggers just made one rush for the ladders, and the officers and families had to wait till things weren't quite so thick.

You never saw such a sight as the deck. The luggage was all coming aboard and being dumped down anywhere and anyhow. The deck was one mass of trunks and suitcases and kitbags and holdalls, all strewn about anyhow and lots of them burst and broken. The diggers were all over the place, singing and chaffing the new arrivals. Stewards were running about like rabbits. I saw a few ship's officers looking as if they had discovered a bad smell. The only people who seemed to know their job were a couple of dozen naval ratings with two or three English naval officers. It was a treat to see the way they marched on board, piled their kit and stood waiting for orders. I can tell you we have had a great respect for the British navy ever since the Dardanelles. You've no idea how much safer we felt if the 'Queen Elizabeth' or the 'Majestic' was putting it over with the fifteen-inch guns or the six-inch shrapnel, and it was wonderful the sense of security the searchlights gave us. The effect of a searchlight, either in defence or attack, on one's mind is very considerable. Also the work of the midshipmen handling the tows of boats and lighters at the Gaba Tepe landing was very inspiring, these boys displaying great courage. I heard afterwards some of the naval officers say that our landing was one of the finest things ever done, and nothing but our fellows' language could do justice to it.

Although we had left London so early, what with the delays on the journey and getting us all on and off the tender, it was now beginning to get dark. I grabbed a steward and told him the number of our cabin and asked him where it was. He said we weren't in his section, but he would find our steward.

'Not on your sweet life,' I said. 'You just take me to my cabin and then you can go and get my steward.'

I am very determined in my quiet way, and the fellow saw I meant what I said, so he took us below. In the passage we collided with a steward coming out of a cabin.

'Here is your man, sir,' said the first steward. I gave him a tip and he looked quite pleased as he went away. Mind you, I think tipping a degrading practice, but it always makes things run smoothly. Our fellows are wonderfully independent and don't like it if you offer them money, but sooner than make trouble they'll usually take it. Our steward showed us into the cabin. It certainly was a fair size, but it was the most bare and depressing I have ever seen. There were two bunks, one against the passage wall and one against the partition, and there was a kind of couch under the porthole. It all looked very bleak and not at all homey. I missed the nice bright curtains and cushions you get on a liner.

I asked the steward his name.

'Catchpole,' he said.

'All right, Catchpole,' I said. 'Now, old man, I want us to understand each other. I am a major and you'll say "sir" to me every time. Also I am senior medical officer on this ship, and if you don't jump to it, I'll have you certified insane. If you look after me properly you'll get a fair deal from me.'

'Thank you, sir,' he said.

As a matter of fact it was all bluff about my being senior Med., and anyone knows an army doctor can't certify one of the ship's crew, but I have a great natural turn for poker, and luckily my bluff wasn't called. As a matter of fact there was one senior to me and one junior.

50

Colonel Bird was a fine old bird and there wasn't much he didn't know about surgery, but unluckily none of us were too good on kiddies. Of course I'd done my midwifery, but apart from that I knew no more about babies than a little common sense and some younger brothers can teach you. It's different now, because I seem to have a kind of understanding of babies, and since I've been in practice in Sydney I've had a certain amount of luck in treating some difficult cases, and in fact I'm shortly going to specialize. You may really say it was those weeks on the 'Rudolstadt' that got me going on the job. Old Dr Bird was a hero with the kiddies, but after all abdominal surgery was his line, and as the other doctor, Captain Lyon, was really a mental specialist, not to speak of as often being sozzled as not, I had to get down to it. You might have thought that with a boatload of officers' families they'd have an experienced kiddies' doctor in charge, but that's where you would have thought wrongly.

So I told Catchpole to wait while I had a good look round the cabin, and then I told him we'd want some more pillows and blankets and another carafe and few more things.

'I'll do my best, sir,' he said, 'but we're a bit short.'

'That's no reason I should do without,' I said. 'I've never yet had a batman that didn't learn to do a bit of scrounging for me, and it isn't too late for you to learn. Now jump to it, and you can collect my luggage off the deck and bring it here right away.'

And I told him exactly what we had and passed him a quid.

'All right, sir,' he said, and I could see he had got the spirit of the thing. 'And dinner's ready whenever you want it.'

So we went off to the saloon. I must say I had expected

little tables, the way you get them on the big liners, but this was no better than the 'Karoola' or the 'Oonah' or any interstate boat. There were three or four long tables down the middle of the saloon and shorter tables sticking out from the wall under the portholes on each side. I was disappointed, because I had counted on a table for my little missis and me, and perhaps a couple of pals. However, it seemed to be first come first served at the moment, so we just sat down in the first place that came handy and started our dinner, when who should we see opposite to us but Larry Sievers.

'Cheerio, old son,' I said. 'Are you coming on this trip?'

But he said no, he was only down there as shipping officer, seeing everything was straight before we left.

'Look, Tom,' he said, 'I can't talk to you now, because I'm having hell's own delight over this business and I must buzz off as soon as I've swallowed this. But I'll come down to your cabin before I go and have a yarn. There are one or two things I want to put you wise to.'

Then he went out and Celia and I finished our dinner. There were kiddies everywhere, all ages, and presently I saw young Dick and Mary. Their father and mother didn't seem to be with them, so when I had finished I went over to them.

'Hullo, Uncle Tom,' said young Dick. 'I've eaten everything on the menu.'

'Well, son,' I said, 'you'll probably be for it in the night. Where are Dad and Mum?'

'Mum's unpacking,' said Mary, 'and she told us to go and get some dinner, and we didn't know which things to have, so we had them all.'

'Dad's on deck,' said young Dick. 'He couldn't find his suitcase, the one that had his German souvenirs, and he's awfully waxy.'

So I told the kids to come along to my cabin if they

wanted a dose in the night, and that made them laugh, and I set them spinning round and round on those fixed chairs, much to the annoyance of some of the women in the saloon. Then I went down to the cabin and found Celia unpacking and Catchpole there talking to her.

'I got all your things, sir,' said Catchpole, 'but it was a job, I tell you, sir, some of the Australian soldiers are a deal too free with other people's property. I had quite a business to get your kitbag, I can tell you. There was a big chap trying to get it open, saying he thought there was beer it it.'

That struck me as very humorous, because the contents of my kitbag were as a matter of fact chiefly bottles. I wished that big chap, whoever he was, had got it open and taken a good swig of iodine. That would have taught him to respect property.

'You didn't happen to see a suitcase of Colonel Fairchild's anywhere about, did you?' I asked him.

'Is Colonel Fairchild a tall big officer, sir, with the baldish head?'

'That's the bird,' I said.

'Well, sir, I saw him engaged in an argument with some of those Australian soldiers. It seems, sir, they thought there was beer in his case.'

'They seem to be thinking of nothing but beer,' said Celia. 'I thought this was a dry ship.'

'That's why,' I said. 'A dry ship means beer in the men's quarters and beer coming on board at every port.'

'They say, sir, in the stewards' quarters,' said Catchpole, 'that those Australian soldiers have brought dozens of cases of beer on board. In fact there was quite a commotion before your train arrived because some of the men who were loading up the tender smashed a couple of cases, and there was a free fight on the wharf. One of our men who happened to be ashore was in it, and he says those Australians are fair terrors with their fists. It made a good deal of ill feeling, sir.'

'Catchpole says it will be all right so long as the prisoners don't get out,' said Celia, who had nearly finished unpacking and had got the cabin wonderfully tidy.

'What do you know about prisoners, Catchpole?' I said.

'Prisoners below in the cells, sir.'

I wanted to find out how much he knew, so I only asked if they had had to crime some of the diggers already.

'Couldn't say as to that, sir. These prisoners came down yesterday by a special train with a guard and were taken straight to the cells.'

'Cripes!' I said.

I had to hear some more about this, so I told Celia to get into bed, for the poor kid looked quite dead to the world, and I'd go up on deck and see what was doing. And I told Catchpole to keep his eyes and ears open and pass me the word if he heard anything among the stewards. Up on deck it was worse than ever. The diggers weren't drunk, but they were a cheery lot and they'd got the beer from somewhere all right, and no one seemed to be keeping any discipline. Some of them were going through the suitcases that had got smashed in the tender, and borrowing anything they wanted. I judged it wasn't the moment to interfere, and anyway Colonel Picking was in command and it was for him to give orders. So I caught a steward and asked for Colonel Fairchild's cabin. He had a bonzer suite on deck for him and his missis and the kiddies, two cabins and a bathroom. Luckily it was on the port side, and when I explain what I mean, as I shall later, you will see why I say 'luckily'. I knocked at the door and Mrs Jerry said 'Come in', so I went in. She was just putting Dick and Mary to bed, so we had a bit of a game, and then I asked her where Jerry was.

'Don't ask me,' said Mrs Jerry. 'He is raging round the ship after the man that pinched his suitcase of souvenirs. I don't suppose he'll ever see it again, but if he does that man will need new teeth and probably a new face. I don't mind much myself, because a ton of old German helmets and revolvers and shell cases aren't going to brighten up the home, but I'm sorry for Jerry, and I'm sorry for all of us till it is found.'

Just then Jerry walked in.

'Well, old son,' I said, 'have the brutal and licentious soldiery been going through your stuff?'

'My God, I'll go through that fellow when I catch him,' said Jerry. 'There was a revolver I got off a Boche at Pozières that I wouldn't lose for anything, and a bit of Richthofen's aeroplane I got when he came down. I was up having a yarn with the Lewis gunners then and saw every darned thing that happened, and now those lousy blighters have pinched it.'

Of course the kiddies yelled out 'lousy blighters!' from the other cabin where they slept with the nurse, and Mrs Jerry told the old man off pretty sharply.

'See here, Jerry,' I said, wishing to change the subject, for if there is one thing I hate it is to be in a family quarrel, one looks such a fool, 'what about these prisoners?'

'Well, what have you heard?' he asked.

'A trainload came down yesterday, by what my steward tells me. They're down below in the cells with a guard.'

Jerry was going to say something, but he got a look from Mrs Jerry that made him shut up.

'Well, all I can say is,' said Mrs Jerry, 'there "would" be prisoners on this boat, and I shall be surprised if we ever reach Adelaide. Get out, both of you. I've got to finish unpacking and get the children to sleep. When do we start?'

But neither of us knew, and as Mrs Jerry was evidently working up for a storm, we just slipped silently away.

'This doesn't seem too bright,' said Jerry. 'Come and have a drink.'

'Lemonade or ginger beer?' I asked in my quiet sarcastic way.

Then Jerry said everything he had been bottling up since Mrs Jerry gave him that look. My oath, there wasn't much he didn't say about dry ships and soft drinks. So we went along to see if we could raise something in the surgery, and in the companion way Catchpole ran into us.

'Excuse me, sir,' he said, 'but Captain Sievers from Headquarters is in your cabin and would like to have a word with you.'

'Come on, Jerry,' I said, 'we'll put old Larry through it and get the dinkum oil on what's happening.'

When we got to the cabin, there was Celia sitting up in her berth with her pretty hair in two plaits, looking like a kid of seventeen, and there was old Larry on the couch under the porthole, looking a bit sheepish. I introduced the old Colonel, and Celia apologized for receiving company in bed, and then we got down to brass tacks.

'Now, you old thief,' I said to Larry, 'what's all this about prisoners? This is a dirty deal you're giving us.'

Larry looked the picture of misery.

'When I suggested you might go on this boat with Mrs Bowen,' he said, 'I hadn't an idea they were going to take prisoners as well as troops.'

So I got some whisky out of my medical stores and we all had one in the tooth-glass.

'Here's fun,' said Jerry. 'Now tell us what the game is.'

'Well,' said Larry, 'H.Q. has unloaded a whole gang of prisoners on us, and I don't suppose there are a worse set of fellows in the whole A.I.F. than this little lot. Some were in for murder and some for theft and some for deserting, and some for other things,' and Larry looked so meaningly at Celia that we all felt quite uncomfortable. 'They're just about the scum of the A.I.F., and lots of them have never seen a day's active service. They joined up as late as they could and saw to it that they spent their time in gaol, finding it a pleasanter proposition than France.'

'I suppose they're locked up, with a guard,' said Jerry.

'The murderers are,' said Larry. 'Some of them had their sentences commuted when they got on board. The really bad hats are in the cells, and I must say I'm sorry for them. It will be like the Black Hole of Calcutta when you get to the Red Sea.'

'Their troubles,' said the old Colonel, 'and I've handled troops before now.'

'Yes, Colonel,' said Larry, 'but you had good officers under you and it was active service. I don't want to be a wowser, but you will want to keep your eyes open. I won't say anything against Picking or his adjutant, but I'd as soon have a couple of school marms on the job.'

'It's a bit of a nark,' I said, thoughtfully thinking it all over.

'Well, don't say I didn't warn you,' said Larry, and he got up and shook hands with Celia.

'I must be buzzing off,' he said. 'Good-bye, Mrs Bowen, and I wish I'd made you go on the "Ormolu".'

We took him down to the surgery and got some medical comforts from Lyon, who was just checking them over. Shortly afterwards old Dr Bird took Lyon's key away, and only he and I had keys to the drug cupboard. It seemed better under the circumstances. Lyon wasn't any too pleasant about it, but the old doctor wasn't taking any insolence, and he put the fear of the Lord into Lyon, so that he never put his face into the surgery again. I heard of him afterwards, up Townsville way, and he got into trouble with the police over a woman that died.

So we saw Larry over the side and I heard the anchor being hauled up, so I turned in. Celia was asleep, and I was glad we were on the lower deck, as the deck cabins were very noisy.

4

Trouble in the Bath

The events of the next few days I shall not be able to describe very well, for we ran into rough weather at once. Celia was not ill, but as the sea was very high and all the doors and windows of the lounge had to be kept shut and no one could get about on deck, she found it more pleasant to stay in the cabin and read, while Catchpole looked after her. There was a stewardess, but she was like most of them, lazy and insolent, not exactly rude, but what in the army is called 'dumb insolence', and Celia fired her the first day and told Catchpole he could take on the job. He and Celia got on wonderfully well. Indeed she was quite a turn for getting on with people and that is partly why she has been such a social success in Sydney, being a member of the Rose Bay Golf Club and going to various other social functions, just as if she had been a Sydney girl. I managed to get about because it was my job, but I felt like a sick cat half the time. Colonel Picking was down, and half the officers and more than half the diggers, and I must say the rest worked like navvies at looking after the sick ones. Jerry was as fit as a fiddle and practically running the ship. Mrs Jerry was pretty bad and so was the nurse, but the two kids enjoyed it all thoroughly and came down to all meals. Indeed they got a bit above themselves, as you will hear later in the matter of the baths.

The second day out I rang for Catchpole to get my

bath, for I hadn't been able to face the bathroom on the first day. No one answered, so I went along to the bath myself. I like a cold plunge in the morning. Some people like a hot bath, but I always feel twice as fresh if I get under the shower. Sometimes I have a good hot bath first and lie soaking in it, and then finish up with the shower. One thing I do miss in your English bathrooms is a shower. In Sydney every house that has a bath at all has a shower. There wasn't a shower in this bath, so I turned on the cold water. Steam began to arise from the bath. It was boiling salt water. I cursed a bit and let the water off and tried the hot tap for a change, and nothing came out at all. I couldn't make it out, so I turned the cold tap on again and ran a little boiling water into the bath. Then I shaved, and by that time the water was just cool enough to stand in it and give myself a kind of sponge down. I couldn't raise Catchpole anywhere, so I went to the saloon as soon as I was dressed, and got a cup of tea and some toast and some eggs and bacon which was about all I felt fit for. The ship was rolling like anything and the line of the horizon through the portholes nearly finished me off, so I quickly got up on deck and as I was staggering along, clinging to the rail, I met one of the ship's engineers. He looked a bit worried. I introduced myself and he said he was the chief engineer. We took a bit of a constitutional round the sheltered part of the deck.

'Queer kind of hot water supply you have on this boat,' I said.

'I know it,' he said – of course he was a Scotsman though his name was Schultz. 'This ship is going to turn my remaining hairs grey. I'll tell you, Major, exactly what has occurred.'

By this time we were opposite the smoke-room door, and out came Jerry, just looking round for someone to strafe. As soon as he saw old Schultz he began to throw fits. I cannot repeat all he said, but it was a treat.

'See here,' he said, shouting with rage, 'what kind of a bastard of a ship do you call this, Mr Schultz? I go to your bloody lavatory and when I pull the plug out comes a lot of scalding steam that fairly takes the skin off————.'

Well, luckily, he didn't finish what he was going to say, because a whole crowd of diggers had come up to hear the row, and when they heard about the hot steam they laughed so they couldn't stop. People say the digger is not appreciative of humour, but he has a wonderful sense of what is really funny and will appreciate a joke wonderfully. No one who had heard that crowd could ever say they hadn't a sense of humour. I must say I couldn't help laughing too, and even old Schultz raised a smile. Then some of the diggers began to sing 'Have you seen the Colonel?' and I leave you to guess what kind of words they put to it. Poor old Jerry was getting angrier every minute, till Schultz said: 'Come away to my cabin, the pair of ye,' so we went along to his cabin and he told us the tale.

It seems that this 'Rudolstadt' used to do the South Atlantic run from Hamburg before the War. After the Armistice the Germans had to hand her over to the British, but before they left her the engineers had connected every pipe up wrong. Hot was cold, cold was waste, waste was boiling, you didn't know where you were.

'We've been working on her for three weeks,' said Schultz, 'and I thought we had her put to rights, but it would appear that we were in error. This voyage, gentlemen, will be far from comfortable. As for the Colonel's misfortune, I can only offer my apologies, and I'll get my men going on the pipes again at once. They Gairmans

61

must have had some verra fine engineers among them. It is a pretty job the way yon pipes are connected.'

'Pretty be damned,' said Jerry. 'How would you like————?'

But even Jerry had to laugh.

'Well, I must be getting to my work,' said Schultz. 'I misdoubt there'll be more trouble before long. I can aye tell from the start when we are to have a mischancy voyage.'

'Cheerful sort of bloke,' said Jerry.

By the time we reached Gibraltar Schultz had got the pipes right, but you could never rely on them. Poor old Schultz raised hell, but the Germans had done their work very thoroughly. Just then he put his head back into the cabin.

'I may as well tell ye now,' he said, 'that we have no refrigerator on board.' And out he went.

Jerry and I went out on deck again. I was being sick all that day at intervals, but quite bright in between. The diggers were still standing about on deck laughing, and a couple of sailors were fixing a rope across from the corner of the lounge aft to the ship's railings, thus roping off the starboard side of the deck.

'What's that for?' I asked one of the sailors.

'Men's side of the deck, sir,' he said.

Jerry and I looked at each other.

'I thought this was all first class,' I said.

'There isn't much room for the troops, sir,' said the sailor, 'and we've had orders to rope off this side of the deck for them.'

'Good morning, Colonel; good morning, Doctor,' said a nasty kind of voice. It was a young officer, the type I very much dislike, with a little black toothbrush moustache and very pleased looking. 'I'm Anderson,' he said, 'Captain Anderson, the Colonel's adjutant.'

'Well, what the hell have you put all those troops under the cabin windows for?' asked Jerry.

'The men found they were cramped for space,' said Anderson in that nasty voice of his. He was a real little counter-jumper, and I could see from the jump he had no guts at all and wouldn't stay the course, and you will hear more of this at a future time. 'So they sent up word to the Colonel they wanted some more deck space and he arranged with Captain Spooner, the ship's captain, that they should have this side of the deck reserved for them.'

'The hell he did,' said Jerry.

I knew what he was thinking, because I was thinking the same thing myself. I could see from that moment onwards what the discipline was going to be. Who ever heard of a C.O. in his senses letting his troops tell him where to allot their quarters? The only other time I've ever come across such a thing was when an American squadron visited Sydney one year, and the flagship came to anchor with half the ship's company yelling up advice to the captain on the bridge, and the marines sat down on guard. Oh, they were a nice lot. Of course the whole thing was a muddle from the beginning. If you carry troops it can only be under strict discipline. I've been from Australia to Egypt and back to Australia, and back again to France, all the way round by the Cape, and there isn't much I don't know about troop-ships. But here was Colonel Picking starting off with giving them whatever they asked for. What it came to was that the officers, their wives, widows, kiddies and whatnots were to have half the promenade deck. The other half of the promenade was reserved – that got me wild, 'reserved' – for the diggers. As for the boat deck, it was so small and so full of lifeboats that you could hardly get a chair in. Also you know the way the couples make for the boat deck in the tropics and how they freeze other people out. I admit it was hard on the diggers, and the quarters they had were a disgrace, but one must have discipline. Once the diggers were allowed on the first-class decks it was all up with discipline. No one could stop them coming over the dividing line, and the noise on the starboard side was like Saturday afternoon in the Domain. Singing, talking, scrapping, mouth-organs, concertinas, and always the voice of the men playing house, calling out the numbers in that dull sing-song till it almost got on your nerves.

Anderson told us the Colonel was calling an officers' meeting at twelve o'clock.

'I don't fancy being bossed about by that little pip-squeak,' I said to Jerry.

Jerry was so sore about the pipes and the troops that he could hardly do justice to it. In the smoke-room I ran across Jack Howe, the fellow in the infantry I had seen on the tender. He said his wife was a very bad sailor and was pretty sick, so I said I'd go down and see her. I did my best for her, but she was one of those unlucky dames that can't stand the slightest motion. There was only the one stewardess for that deck and she was pretty busy that morning, so I went in to tell Celia and when she heard there might be another chance of getting in on the stewardess, she got up and went over to little Mrs Howe to see if she could help.

I went up to the officers' meeting, but as most of them weren't there, we didn't get much done. Colonel Picking presided, but he looked like a drowned kitten. Anderson did most of the talking. Hours of duty for the officers were arranged and the usual routine. I didn't have to go on duty, of course, for I had my own surgery hours, but I knew that Howe or one of the junior officers would be glad of a helping hand occasionally. As for Anderson, I may as well say now that I had no use for him. He hadn't joined the A.I.F. till 1917, being then twenty-four, and had managed never to see a day's fighting, but he got his captaincy all right. He was well in with the Horseferry Road lot, and knew how to wangle things for himself well enough, but he hadn't the first idea how to handle men. He would give an order, and if the men didn't jump to it he would nag at them like a schoolteacher. Of course they sized him up at once, and sometimes they called him Andy and sometimes Nancy – more preferably the latter. I must say the digger is a wonderful judge of character. Now Jerry was nearly as bald as an egg and had the devil's temper and would roar them up good and proper, but the men would do anything for him. Many's the time Anderson got into a fix by giving an order that no one took any notice of, and then he would come to me or Jerry. I could nearly always reason with the boys, and Jerry would curse their heads off in a friendly way, and then they would say 'Good-oh, Doc' or 'Have it your own way, Colonel', and go off and do it as mild as lambs. One of the first rules in the army is, never give an order unless you are sure it will be carried out. I have seen many an officer come to grief that way.

Anyway, Picking said there would be another meeting at twelve the day after, and he hoped more officers would be able to attend. So I went back to the cabin, but Celia was gone. The sea was beginning to go down a bit and we could see the coast of Spain or Portugal, so I went in to lunch. I found Celia there. Our seats were together at one of the long tables, at the head of which was Schultz, though he but rarely showed up for meals, for which I don't blame him, for he came in for a lot of ragging about those pipes. Next to Celia was the Fairchild family, and next to me were Jack Howe and his wife, so we made a nice little party. Opposite us was

the C. of E. padre with his wife and two kids, and an
old tabby called Miss Johnson travelling alone. How
she got on that boat beats me, but I should think she
could have travelled all round the world in great safety.
And there was a bright little woman called Mrs Dick,
but everyone called her Mrs Dicky. No one knew much
about her except that she had been on the stage and
hadn't got her husband with her, though she talked of
him very affectionately. She was very cheery and kept
things alive. The Old Man, Captain Spooner, took quite
a liking to her and wanted her to come and sit at his
table, but she liked to stay where she was. The Fairchilds
and the Howes and ourselves got into the habit of
treating all our seats alike, and anyone would drop into
any empty chair, so that one never knew who one would
be sitting next to or opposite to, which made things a
little less monotonous.

Celia told me how she had been to see Jack Howe's
wife and had washed her face and hands and brushed her
hair and tidied up a bit in the cabin and given her Eno's
Fruit Salts. Of course, give me Eno's on a rough voyage
and you won't get me to take it – it would be simply
asking for trouble – but some appreciate it. Celia was
quite upset about Mrs Howe's cabin. It was one of
those inside cabins and they had to have the electric light
on all day, and it was pretty stuffy already. What it
would be like in the tropics was a nasty thought,
especially as the opposite wall was the engine room and
mostly too warm to enjoy. Also Celia had had a good
old turn-up with the stewardess, which had done her a
lot of good.

After lunch I got Celia tucked up in a chair on deck
to enjoy the fresh air while I went down to Colonel
Bird, to see how things were below. The men's quarters
were pretty crowded. There was only one decent sized

cabin on the deck below ours. It was aft, and was to be used for a surgery for the lower deck. Also it was the storeroom for drugs and bandages and for the food for the babies. There were tins and tins of powdered and condensed milk, and scales to weigh the kiddies. One of the sergeants had done part of his dental training in Melbourne, and he was able to do any emergency dentistry we needed. It was of a rough and ready kind, but if a digger wanted a tooth out, he could always get a couple of pals to hold him down. He couldn't do much about stoppings, and even less false teeth. Lyon had some false teeth, but one night when he was pretty tight he took them out to show a friend, and then tried to shut them up in his cigarette case. Considerable damage was done all round. The cigarette case was never the same again, and poor old Lyon had to eat with his front teeth, for all the world like a rabbit, all the way from Port Said.

Our cabins may have been crowded, but the men's quarters were ten times as bad. There wasn't a corner where a bunk hadn't been squeezed in, and how they managed to keep their kit in any kind of order beats me. Also the borrowing habits of the digger came into operation here, and when the officer of the day made his rounds, more than half his time was taken up with complaints about things that had been pinched. It wasn't so bad while they only borrowed among themselves, for the digger has a great sense of give and take. Our fellows are wonderfully generous and will do anything for a cobber who is down on his luck, and equally they will help themselves to anything they want. It all comes out pretty straight in the long run, and the less notice you take of it the better. But when they began to borrow elsewhere it was more serious, and that was what started the trouble after Colombo, to which we shall come later on.

The surgery, being aft, was well lighted with port-holes, also with windows on to the deck. I may as well say at once that I am not very accurate as regards the names of different parts of a ship, but shall do my best to make things clear. As you will have already gathered, there was a small boat deck, then a promenade deck with officers and families on the port side and diggers on the starboard side. The lounge, smoke-room and bar were on this deck, if you can call it a bar where you can only get soft drinks, as were a few cabins with bathrooms. On the next deck below, C deck, were the officers' cabins and the saloon and the first-class surgery. Below this were two more decks. The upper one, or D deck, was officers' cabins on the starboard side and men's quarters on the port side, and there was the lower deck surgery and a galley. The lowest deck, or E deck, was also men's quarters, and here were the cells, so-called. The ship's crew were forward and the naval ratings aft. You may see that the men were as thick on the ground as sand hoppers at Manly beach.

The troops had access to the well deck of course at each end of their deck. Where the cargo hatch would normally have been, a great wooden grating had been placed, to give more air to the lowest deck, and by God it was wanted. It wasn't so bad at first, because the weather was cold, but after we were through the Canal you will hear more of it.

I spent most of one day going through the surgery stores with Colonel Bird. They were pretty well stocked and the orderly seemed to know his job. I had a good look around the locker where the prepared food for the babies was kept.

'How many kiddies do we feed here?' I said to the old doctor.

'About ten,' he said, 'and lucky if it isn't twelve before the end of the voyage.'

Well, I didn't know much about babies, but I have a mathematical turn of mind, and I studied up the doses on the tins, and I nutted it out that we weren't any too well off for patent foods. So I asked Colonel Bird, but he said it was all right. I could have kicked myself later for not standing up to him, but he was an older man, and I had done nothing but my midwifery. If I'd known that he'd hardly so much as touched a kiddie since he left the hospital, I'd have spoken up a bit more. Well, we had no deaths.

While I was checking over the medical comforts, a fellow came up to me.

'Here, Doc,' he said, 'can you come down to a bloke in the cells?'

'What's up?' I asked.

'He had a bit of turn-up with the military policeman and stoushed him,' said the man, who was a corporal.

So I got some things together and went down. It did strike me that the man who was stoushed might need some attention too. It was the first time I had been on to the lowest deck. I spent plenty of time there later, and I disliked it just as much the more I saw of it. The ports had to be kept shut as often as not when there was a bit of a sea, and the only air they seemed to get was along the passage from the doors on to the well deck, and even then the air had to come down through the grating I told you of. And if it was rough the waves would sometimes come slopping through that grating and the doors had to be kept shut. Talk of the monkey house. I've had a good many smells to put up with in my time. Hospital ships and clearing stations soon kill or cure you of any squeamish feelings, but that lower deck was the limit. I felt really sorry for the diggers, some of them quite decent chaps, shut up in that stinking hole. No wonder they wanted a bit of the promenade deck where they could see some sky and breathe a bit. They ought to have had the whole boat, except just for officers' quarters. The people who were to blame were the dod-blasted buggers at Horseferry Road who put families and troops together on a small ship, unsuitable for a long voyage, with a lot of officers who didn't know the first thing about troops. Mind you, I've never yet met the men I couldn't handle. To begin with I'm six foot two and pretty good with my fists, and though I have a wonderfully quiet way with the men, they soon know who is top dog. But except for Jerry and Jack Howe and three or four others, you might as well have put a special constable in charge of Flemington on Cup Day. Half the troops were the biggest crooks and toughs in the A.I.F., and it didn't give the decent ones much of a chance. Some of them stuck to us. If they hadn't the ship would have been even worse than it was. The sergeants were just as bad, except again for the few exceptions. Somehow a bad sergeant is one of God's nastiest creations.

I can only say that I wouldn't have shut a dog up in the places they called cells. If the men who were shut up there had been sensitive kind of chaps, they would have gone right off their nuts, but luckily for them they weren't. If you've ever been over Port Arthur, or read 'For the Term of his Natural Life', you'll know a bit about the way convicts were treated in those olden days. You might have thought you were on a convict ship the way these poor fellows were in close confinement in holes you could hardly turn round in, hardly lighted, and with no fresh air. They were supposed to be taken out for exercise regularly, but as you will see, they didn't all appreciate it, and a lot of them refused to go out at all. They had the wind up the guards from the start, and by the time we were in the Red Sea, the guards jumped to it every time a prisoner opened his mouth. Of course I didn't know all this at the beginning, but it began to be clear all too soon.

The corporal took me to one of those Black Holes and unlocked the door. We were only three days out, but the stink fairly caught me.

'Well, what's up?' I asked.

'Bust me bloody thumb,' said the man inside. He was sitting on his bunk smoking, and where he got the cigarettes from you could have searched me, but there was nothing those blokes couldn't get. They reminded you of the Kelly gang in many ways, the way a few of them got to terrorize practically the whole of the ship's company.

'How did you do that?' I asked, being rather curious.

'Bloody M.P. came to take me for a walk. I told the bastard I wasn't going, and he started in arguing, so I stoushed the bloody sod in the jaw and bust me thumb,' said the man, spitting in a nasty way.

Well, I may as well say here that I shall not repeat the word bloody as often as I heard it, for it is not a literary word and does no good. But you may take it that those fellows just used it and other similar words in one long sweet song. I don't know if you know a poem called the 'Australaise', which I think is by C. J. Dennis and begins somewhat as follows:

> Fellows of Australia,
> Blokes and coves and coots,
> Get a —— move on
> Shift your —— boots
> Gird yer —— loins up
> Get yer —— gun
> Set the —— enemy
> And watch the ——s run

71

and is of course sung to the tune of 'Onward Christian Soldiers'. Well, if you do, you will know what I mean. And if you don't, it will give you some idea. I am wonderfully wide-minded in many ways, but I do think there are times when you should not use bad language. Old Jerry could hold his own against any two diggers, but he reserved it for suitable occasions and didn't just leave the tap running as you might say.

'You come along to the surgery,' I said. 'I can't see down here.'

The corporal started in to interfere and said he daren't let the prisoner out.

'You'll damn well do as I tell you,' I said. 'Where's the sergeant?'

The fellow went along to get the sergeant. I can size people up pretty quickly and one look at that sergeant told me he was the right sort.

'What's your name?' I asked.

'Higgins, sir,' said he, and saluted smartly.

'Bring O'Donovan here to the surgery,' I said.

'Aw, spare me days,' said the prisoner, 'my moniker's Cavanagh.'

'I'm not surprised,' I said, 'and whenever there's trouble in poor old Aussie your family and friends are at the bottom of it.'

Cavanagh was starting in to argue, but Higgins shut him up quick and lively and marched him off to the surgery, with the corporal on the other side. When we got up there I had a look at his thumb. He had dislocated it.

'I'll have to pull this straight, Cavanagh,' I said. 'You'll have to stick it.'

'Aw, I'll stick it, Doc,' he said. 'Only tell that son of a bitch of a corporal to stand off, or I'll spoil his dial with me other hand.'

72

As he seemed to have a prejudice against the corporal
I told the sergeant to stand by while I got Cavanagh's
thumb in place. He never seemed to feel it, but just
went on cursing all the time. There is something about
swearing that seems to take the place of an anaesthetic
sometimes. When I'd finished and got his hand strapped
up I said:

'What happened to the M.P. you stoushed?'

'He's crying for his mammy,' said Cavanagh, and it
was the first time I had seen a pleasing expression on his
face, 'and serve him right, the bleeding Protestant.'

'All right, you dirty Mick,' said the corporal. 'I'll smash
your bloody crust for you when we get to Sydney.'

'I expect his jaw is broken, sir,' said Higgins quite
quietly. And then he jumped on the corporal and roared
him up well and truly, and sent him off to find the
military policeman. He wasn't long. The man's jaw
wasn't broken, but he had lost three teeth and would
have a face like a bit of bad meat in a few hours. Well,
I talked to them all like an uncle from Holland, and I
ordered Cavanagh back to his cell under guard, and told
Higgins to report to me again.

'Aren't you going to give me some medical comforts,
Doc?' said Cavanagh.

'The Major is not,' said Higgins.

'To hell with the pope,' said the corporal, and they
ran Cavanagh out of the surgery before he could say
any more.

'I tell you honest, Doc,' said the man who had lost
three teeth, 'this job gets the wind up me. These prisoners
are fair demons. I'd rather be back on the Peninsula, or
on a Saturday night down Little Lon.'

So we got yarning about old times, as I had done a bit
of prospecting down Little Lonsdale Street, to give it its

full name, myself, though it had never had much appeal for me. The way the Janes sit at their doors waiting for you takes away all the romance. When he found I'd been on the Peninsula he brightened up and I told him to keep his head and let me know if there was any trouble.

'Right oh, Doc,' said he, 'but I'll not go near that Mick again without the sergeant.'

So he went off and Higgins came in.

'Now, Sergeant,' I said, 'let's have the dinkum oil on this.'

It turned out that Higgins had been in the old New South Wales Mounted Police and in the South African war. He was quite a middle-aged man and he knew what discipline was. My oath, when I think what Higgins did for us later. He was a decent little chap, and I am glad to say he is doing quite well up Goulburn way.

'I don't like this rough house, Sergeant,' I said.

'Nor me, sir,' said Higgins. 'From what I've seen of these fellows we'll have a good deal more. They have got the wind up the guards good and proper and threaten all sorts of things. You know, sir, the way I look at it, lots of these fellows haven't seen much service and they get scared easily. We've a number of old-timers among us who were through the Peninsula and France, but they don't want to come back to their wives as casualties after getting away with it from the Turk and the Hun. It isn't in human nature, and if those men are on guard they aren't going to take any risks. Take my word, sir, the officers will get very little backing from the men. I don't like to say it, for I'm an old soldier myself, but there it is.'

'And let me tell you, Sergeant,' I said, 'that as far as I can see, the men are going to get damned little backing from the officers.'

'Thank you, sir,' said Higgins. 'We all know old P. and S., if you'll excuse me saying so, sir, and most of us know all we want to know about the adjutant.'

I could see Higgins was a white man, and though none is more strict on military discipline than I am, I could see that this was one of the times when human feelings would have to come first. I had a long yarn with Higgins, first shutting the windows and putting a notice on the door to say the surgery was closed for half an hour, and trusting to luck that neither Bird nor Lyon, who was not yet in disgrace, would come down. We nutted it all out like this. I knew four or five officers besides myself whom I could thoroughly trust, and hoped there might be a few more. Higgins said half the troops were ordinary decent felows, but would follow the hot-heads. About twenty were real bad eggs, ready for anything, and to them we must add the prisoners who had been set free on board, and those – mostly murderers – who were still in the cells, but had frightened the guard into letting them talk to their friends and get cigarettes and drink, and were practically free men. And the rest, he said, would go with the bad lot just for the lark. As for the N.C.O.'s, they were much the same. A few trustworthy men, some crooks, and a lot that would follow the crooks from fear, or for the fun of the thing. There was nothing to be done about it, but Higgins said he would pass the word along to me if things looked any worse.

It was a great disappointment to all that we didn't put in at Gibraltar, nor Marseilles, nor Naples, nor Malta. I had quite looked forward to a trip ashore, but we went right on down the Mediterranean. I must say there is something wonderfully impressive about the African coast as seen from the sea. The sun began to come out and all sorts of people came up on deck that we had never seen before. Most of the wives were English girls, and there were two French ones. Ten of them had young babies and the fathers were wonderfully good in looking after the kiddies and carrying them about on deck when the mothers were too sick to look after them. Every day I had a kind of nursery party in the surgery when the babies were brought down for their bottles. I became quite handy at mixing the food and warming it on a spirit lamp, and often I used to give some of the kids their bottles. It was all good practice, I thought at the time. Well, things don't always happen as we mean, and anyway my time on the 'Rudolstadt' taught me something about kiddies, so I have that to be thankful for, even if it is other people's kiddies. They were rum little beggars and I got to be quite fond of them and quite took it to heart when they didn't put on weight. Mostly they did pretty well on that part of the trip. There was one baby girl I had a special fondness for, a jolly little kid of five months who always had a laugh for me. The diggers used to crowd round the surgery to see the kiddies, and would take turns at nursing them if the mother was busy.

All was going fairly well till we past the heel of Italy, when a wind came down the Adriatic that fairly laid us all out. All those who had been sick before were for it again, and those who hadn't now got what was coming to them. Luckily Celia and I kept pretty fit and we did what we could for others. Celia was wonderful with little Mrs Howe, going every day to her cabin to cheer her up, and getting her up on deck when she could. However, when we got under Crete we were sheltered from the wind and next day everyone came down to breakfast. I noticed the old tabby, Miss Johnson, looking pretty sour that morning, but I was so used to that that I didn't do anything about it, beyond saying good morning. Presently she leaned over the table at me and said:

'Do you know, Major Bowen, what those children have been doing?'

'Search me,' I said, for you never know what kiddies have been up to.

'They climbed up the partition in the ladies' bathroom and looked over into my bath,' she said, 'and I shall have to report it to the captain if you don't punish them.'

'You'd better tell their parents,' I said.

'Aren't they your children, then?' she said.

'Good Lord, no,' I said. Then the humour of the situation struck me so much that I had to begin to laugh. After all the kiddies were only kiddies, and what harm it could do to look at a skinny old maid in her birthday clothes, I don't know. Of course it isn't everyone's taste, and certainly wouldn't have been mine, but the kiddies weren't old enough to know better. She looked as if she would have liked to bite my head off, but for the life of me I couldn't keep from laughing. The story of course got all round the ship and many a good laugh was had. When Mrs Jerry heard what the kiddies had been up to, she told them off, but it took more than that to get young Dick and Mary down. Also there was considerable ill feeling between Mrs Jerry and the old maid for some time. I must say I didn't laugh so much when, in the Red Sea, those two young devils bolted all the lavatory doors from the inside and then crept out under the doors – you know the way those doors in a ship are about a foot from the floor. The stewards had to climb over, or wiggle in, to get them unbolted again, and the two kids were not popular for the next few days. But what can you expect from kiddies? We were just as bad.

One morning early I looked through my porthole and saw a kind of fringe of palm trees across it, so I knew it was Port Said. We tied up soon after breakfast, not far from the mole, and looked forward to going ashore. But

77

at ten o'clock a notice was put up to say women and civilian passengers could go on shore for the day, but there was no leave for officers or troops. I was as wild as a meat-axe. I had been looking forward to showing Port Said to my little missis and buying her some things at Simon Artz's. However, she fixed up to go with Mrs Jerry and the kiddies and Mrs Howe, and off they went in a row-boat. I went down to the surgery to do the morning's routine. Higgins came in and saluted.

'Well, Sergeant,' I said, 'more dirty work at the crossroads?'

'That's right, sir,' he said. 'The men are all going ashore and some of the prisoners have gone too.'

'What in the hell is the Colonel doing?' I asked.

This I know I should not have asked, for I am a great stickler for discipline, but Higgins was an old soldier and knew the game, which was more than the Colonel did, and anyway the Colonel wasn't there.

Higgins grinned.

'He's holding an officers' meeting, sir, to decide what to do.'

'That'll do,' said I. 'Next case.' And for about an hour I was pretty busy with sore fingers, trench feet and other troubles which I will not mention and which an excursion to Port Said would probably not improve. It was stifling hot. All the ship was shut up for coaling. Nowadays the liners all take in oil from the tanks lower down, but we only burnt coal and we were tied up just below the landing stage. The gangways were all out, and the Gippos were going up and down to the portholes with little baskets of coal on their heads, singing a dismal kind of tune. I wouldn't have been below trimming the bunkers for something. Coal dust was sifting in everywhere. You breathed it in with every breath and you couldn't touch a thing without getting black. The orderly had left a tin of babies' food open and there was thick coal dust on it, and I went for him bald-headed. I was sorry for those poor fellows in the cells, but reflecting that most of them weren't there, I soon stopped. The saloon was fairly empty for lunch, which was a change, for we were having two sittings at lunch and dinner every day. But with nearly all the wives and kiddies and the few civilian passengers ashore, there was plenty of room to sit where you liked. I sat next to the English naval officer who was in command of the ratings. His name was Stone, a lieutenant he was, a short, stout, cheery fellow, and he had a second in command called Anstruther. I've never struck a man with such luck as Anstruther. Whatever he touched was lucky. He won the sweep on the ship's run about three times a week. He couldn't pick up a poker hand without four aces in it. When we went on shore at Fremantle he went up to the pony races at Perth and won fifty pounds. Stone lifted his elbow too often, but he was a good sort. They were both pretty fed up at being on the 'Rudolstadt'. I couldn't blame them. Their men and our men weren't on speaking terms, except at the boxing competitions, to which I shall come later. Some of our bad eggs had tried to go through the naval ratings' quarters and had been well and truly told off. But I found that Stone and Anstruther had been in the Dardanelles, so we had much in common and had a good yarn about old days. Stone had been in the old T.B.D. 'Colne' that helped to cover our landing at Gaba Tepe on May 4th. They asked me to their cabin and I found they had a case of whisky and were quite ready to help in putting it down.

So then Stone said he would get his men to do our washing. This was a real godsend, for there was considerable difficulty about the washing. The Captain's orders were that no washing was to be done in the cabins, but of that no one took any notice, as you may well imagine. Naturally all the mothers with kiddies were washing half the time and most of the cabins looked like the back yard on Monday. The diggers had a kind of laundry and were coining money by taking in washing, but they hadn't much idea of it. They had rigged up some lines across the well deck and hung the things up to dry, and it was as good as a play to see all the things hanging out with the wind puffing them out, and to hear what the diggers were saying. It was not very literary and I shall not repeat it, but you may imagine that the sight of half a dozen pairs of pants blowing in the wind caused much amusement, even if not of a very refined kind. However, I arranged with Stone that one of his ratings would come twice a week and fetch our things, so we had as much clean stuff as we wanted all through the voyage. I am wonderfully particular about being clean in every way. A lot of officers got into very bad habits on the voyage. The poker school, as we called them, who were all day long in the smoke-room, mostly didn't wear collars at all when we got past the Canal, and they had their shirt-sleeves rolled up and wore shorts. But though I believe in being comfortable and do not believe in a man's being all dolled up or wearing a boiled shirt, yet I feel a certain respect is owing to women, and I had a clean collar every day, besides shaving regularly.

Also Schultz had now got the pipes fixed up properly and Catchpole got me my bath every morning, and I often got a sponge down before dinner too, which was not official, as we had notice to be careful with the water. It was this day, while at Port Said, that we had trouble with the pipes again and the lavatories all got choked up, which was a great mistake. The Old Man gave Schultz hell over it, and the diggers gave everybody hell, till Schultz said he would connect up the pipes the sailors used for washing down the decks with the boiling salt water, and turn it on them. He got it all right before we left Port Said that night, and as all the women were on shore much trouble was spared, but old Schultz said if ever he met a German engineer again he'd chuck him down the main sewer. Schultz was actually an Australian Scotsman, coming from Brisbane, where they had no sewage system but only septic tanks, so naturally he was a bit self-conscious on the subject. When the diggers found this out they had another song, 'Have you seen the drain-pipe?' They had a great sense of humour, but the words were unsuitable.

All day long the Gippos were going up and down those gangways. You couldn't call it singing, the noise they were making, but it went on all day, and the men were playing house on the promenade deck, and the voice of the fellows calling out the numbers was nearly as bad as the Gippos. It began to get dark and the big searchlights were mounted on the front of the ship. Presently Celia, Mrs Jerry and the kiddies came back, having had a very happy day. They had had lunch at an hotel and taken the kids along the breakwater and then tea at another hotel, besides doing a lot of shopping at Simon Artz. Mrs Jerry had got topees for the kids to wear in the tropics and Celia had got me some khaki silk shirts. She is a thoughtful little woman, and I greatly appreciated those shirts when the hot weather came along.

The ship was like Broken Hill after a dust-storm, only it was coal instead of sand, and the kiddies were black all over in two minutes. Young Dick got mislaid and I found him on the boat deck, in a lifeboat, looking like a Gippo. I got him out and spanked him and took him down to Mrs Jerry. The cabins were all shut up still, and the heat was terrific, and there was no water for

the baths, because we took in salt water for them, and
the water at Port Said, though salt, was not suitable.
Here the Old Man was right. If I knew that a Gippo,
with flies round his eyes and anything you like to think
of on the rest of him had been near any water, I'd give
that water a week to get over it.

So Mrs Jerry went right off the handle and ticked
Catchpole off, not that it was his fault, and finally he
pinched some jugs of water from the Captain's private
supply and the nurse got the kids washed and put to
bed.

Celia and I got some dinner and I introduced her to
Stone and Anstruther. Later on we went up on to the
boat deck. One of the deck stewards, a nice old fellow we
called Daddy, got a rag and cleaned up a bit of the rail
so that we could lean over and watch what was going on.
It was a bonzer night. The coaling had at last stopped
and the sailors were washing down a bit. Away behind us
was the old Europe where I had seen so much. Gallipoli,
Sed-el-Bahr, Gaba Tepe, the British battleships, France,
Pozières, Bullecourt, Villers Bret, St Quentin, Salisbury
Plain, London, Leeds, all gone into yesterday. I'm glad
I saw them, but I don't want to see them again. Good
old Aussie will do me every time. On the right was Port
Said where I had done my dash in the early days of the
Canal fighting in '14. All its lights looked very pretty
under the dark sky. I thought of the shops there, little
scent shops where they offer you a cup of coffee and
something else if you want it, curio shops where you get
your eyes opened about certain things, the mean hotels
that the skirts invite you to, the funny back streets
where I've seen things I wouldn't have believed. A couple
of troopships homeward bound from India had tied up
a little further down, and the men were singing such

popular songs as 'Over there' and 'Three hundred and sixty-five Days'. All their ports were lighted up and they looked liked floating palaces. Little boats were going up and down with lights at the bows and stern, motor boats and row-boats. Dozens of our fellows were coming off from shore with Gippos to row them, all laden with parcels. Simon Artz must have been pretty well cleaned out that day, not to speak of all the little shops. Most of the diggers seemed to be a bit merry. We watched one boatload come alongside. There were six diggers, with two Gippos. When they got near the ship there was a row about the fare. I saw one man by the light of the big arc lamp and recognized him as Cavanagh.

'Ten shillings, Mr Macpherson,' said the Gippo.

'Ten shillings your foot,' said Cavanagh. 'Here's half a dollar, Johnny. Napoo. Mafeesh.'

The Gippos pulled away again from the ship and went on asking for ten shillings. You can't get a Gippo to see that honesty pays. About the time they had got down to eight and sixpence, two of the diggers knocked them into the bottom of the boat and took the oars to row back to the ship. Of course as no leave had been given there were no ladders out from the men's quarters, but their friends on board seemed to have plenty of rope. Cavanagh was standing up in the bows with his back to the ship, telling the world he wasn't going to be cheated by a bloody Turk, when the boat hit the ship with a whack and he fell into the water. All his cobbers in the boat reached over to pull him out, and most of them, being pretty tight, managed to fall in after him. The Gippos got up, and I saw them go through the pockets of the remaining men, who were quite dead to the world. Then they tipped them out and rowed away. I haven't seen such a commotion since the day the leave train was turned back for the last offensive, and our boys finished the journey on the roof of the train because they had left nothing inside to sit on. Half the ship's company were hanging over the edge giving good advice. The diggers that were sober were swimming around, tying ropes on to the ones that were too drunk to look after themselves. The digger is a wonderful swimmer, especially the Sydney men, and here they hadn't any sharks to look out for. I remember at Coogee beach, before they put up a look-out, seeing a man brought out with both legs nipped off by a shark. He looked a bit upset. They say you feel nothing till you come out the water, but I wouldn't like to put my money on it.

Anyway they got all the men on board, and by that time the noise was so bad I thought we'd have the Port Police down on us, so I told Celia to buzz off to bed and I went to find Jerry. He and Jack Howe had joined the poker school in the smoke-room and hadn't heard the row. That is to say, they weren't on duty that evening, so they had no wish to take on other people's troubles. I passed the word to them to come out, as there appeared to be some mis-understanding going on, and told them what had been happening.

'Where's the Colonel?' I asked.

'In bed, I suppose,' said Jerry. 'Nancy has been dancing about on the lower deck telling the men he'd fetch the Colonel, till one of them picked him up by the seat of his pants and put him out. Then he went to bed too. The men have been bringing beer on board all day.'

'Who is down there now?' I asked.

'Search me,' said Jerry. 'It's the Colonel's job, not mine. If he comes and gives an order, I'll carry it out.'

Well, anyway we went down, because we thought we'd better. There was Cavanagh, pretty sober by now, telling the diggers exactly what he thought of the Gippos and the Colonel and the Adjutant and a few more. Jerry and I listened in admiration, for Cavanagh had us cold as far as language went. Then up came little Higgins, as cool as if he was on parade, and snapped out:

'Prisoner, 'shun!'

And will you believe it, Cavanagh just said 'Christ!' and went off to his cell as quiet as a lamb.

'Can you beat it?' I said, and off I went to see that he got some dry clothes. But Higgins was seeing to that all right, and when I left them Cavanagh was trying to kiss Higgins good night. As I say, there is no harm in the digger if you take him the right way. I went back to the well deck and found Jerry had the situation well in hand.

'Now you'd better go to bed, boys,' said Jerry, 'or you'll be losing your beauty sleeps.'

Well, a lot of the things the diggers said wouldn't bear repeating, but they had had their day out and all the beer they wanted, and they went off by twos and threes, quite peacefully. We all went back to the smoke-room and had some ginger ale.

'Ginger ale to drink, and an old woman to command,' said Jack Howe.

'And Nancy to run the errands,' I said.

'Well, God bless Higgins,' said Jerry and then Stone and Anstruther coming in, we finished up in their cabin. About midnight I went up alone to the boat deck. The ship was moving quietly along the canal, with the searchlight making everything very black and white on the banks. The diggers were singing quite melodiously now, 'Annie Laurie' and 'Loch Lomond', and it sounded pretty. The canal stretched away in front with that look it always has of curving away over the edge of the world, reminding me of some lines of Tennyson I once read and cannot remember. And then I saw what many will say you don't see till you are in the Red Sea, but that is just want of observation, namely the Southern Cross. I thought of waking Celia to show it her, but I then thought I wouldn't, so I went quietly down and got to bed.

5

The three-berth-cabin Joke

When I came on deck next morning I found that we weren't far down the Canal. We had tied up soon after midnight and had only just begun to move again. It was a wonderfully peaceful day. The diggers were as pleased as anything by their day ashore and had mostly settled down quietly. Some of them were hanging over the rails, chiacking the Gippos and the Arabs on the banks. It was a lovely sunny day and I can tell you it was good-oh to feel the sun in one's bones again. Jerry and I got quite sentimental, passing the scenes of the Canal fighting. I could point out the very place where the sappers – 3rd Field Company I think it was – put a temporary bridge over the Canal. It was a smart piece of work too. It was like old times to see the line of trees along the Sweet Water Canal, and Ismailia on the other bank. When we were there in '14, Ismailia was just a little township, but now I believe it is a large place with a railhead. Things do change.

A few more passengers had come on at Port Said, though how and where they were fitted in you can search me. There was a Mrs Henley, a big handsome kind of woman, on her way to join her husband in China. She was only going as far as Colombo, where she had to change boats. She had a wonderful deck chair, a kind of cane and bamboo affair with an awning that you could lie or sit in. This she had brought up on to the boat deck, and spent most of her time there. Then there was a man who seemed to be a great pal of hers who came on board at the same time. He was an officer in the Indian army, so he told us, going to Australia for some reason or other. He was a queer fellow. A story got round in the smoke-room, the way these things do, that he had been captured by Afghans up on the North-West frontier and tortured, which had affected his mind a bit. One never knows the truth, and it is surprising the way things get about, starting no one knows where, but he certainly was a bit queer. A big man he was, about my height and build, very light on his feet. This is also like me, for I have always been a bit of a boxer and I have sometimes very much surprised people by the quick way I can move around if necessary. He was always around Mrs Henley. I can't remember his name now but if I call him Smith that will do. 'No names, no pack drill', is a good motto. Some of the officers' wives tried to get off with him, but he didn't so much as look at anyone but Mrs Henley. The only other new passengers were a couple of priests going to Colombo. Frenchmen they were, great big chaps with long black beards. They chummed up with the R.C. padre.

I am a chap that does not say very much, but I do a lot of quiet thinking at times. I was brought up Church of England, and these fancy religions have no appeal for me, but there are occasions on which I have thoroughly appreciated some of the R.C. padres. They were A1 in France, and lots of our boys used to go to mass because they respected the padre and wanted to do him a good turn. One batman I had, a Methodist he was, used to turn up regularly for mass, bringing six or seven R.C.'s with him who weren't as keen as they should be, just to give the padre a better audience. Our padre on this ship, Father Glennie, was one of the whitest men I've ever met. Many's the yarn I've had with him on deck at night. Most of the bad eggs were Irish of course, but if only Father Glennie had been in command, we should have had very little trouble. It often used to get me worried the way the Irish and the R.C.'s seem to stick together. I had a yarn to Father Glennie about it one night.

'Look, Padre,' I said, 'why doesn't the Pope send some decent R.C. padres to Australia, that could pull with the government and make their people a bit more patriotic?'

Then he explained to me that the Pope hadn't much say in the matter, because Australia was an Irish mission.

'Well, God help Australia,' I said.

Father Glennie laughed. He had a kind of a liking for me, and he was that kind of a chap you could say anything to, not like some parsons I have known.

'See here, Padre,' I said, 'I don't mind being the mug. If I wrote a letter to the Pope, explaining that we Australians don't want a lot of Mick bastards with their ugly long upper lips coming preaching sedition, do you think he'd ever get it?'

But the padre said he thought not.

We had a great old yarn about it, and I could see that he agreed with me, though of course he couldn't say so. I'd have gone to mass any day to please Father Glennie, though quite aware that it is a mistake, and not liking to do anything without my breakfast. There was nothing in the world he was afraid of, and if it hadn't been for him, Sergeant Higgins would have had his brains knocked out with a bottle and been feeding the sharks long ago. He wasn't any too strong either, and hardly any flesh on his bones, but nothing could stop him from his work. We used to have a song at school:

Catholic dogs,
Jump like frogs

which we always yelled at the Micks. I didn't know what

89

the words meant then, and I don't now, but the idea is all right. There's one thing: a parson and a doctor have much in common, and that is very likely why Father Glennie and I got to be such good pals.

By tea time we were as far down as the Bitter Lakes. The sun made the desert away to the east all pink and yellow. There is something about the desert very unlike anything else. I used to love those early days on the Canal, when we got over on the east side, and the nights were frosty and bright and the days hot, and you saw the old desert stretching into the distance for ever. It gets a fellow thinking somehow.

Celia and Mrs Dicky were sitting on the boat deck, looking at the view, when I joined them, and we chatted a bit. One of the officers, Lieutenant Starkie his name was, was sitting not far off with his wife, one of the French girls. He was a weedy-looking fellow who had been an accountant before the War. She was a dark girl, not very tall but a good figure and black eyes. I only knew them by sight. Starkie used to come on deck nearly every morning with huge teeth marks on his neck, and naturally there had been a good deal of comment. When Starkie saw me, he came over to where I was sitting.

'Can I have a word with you, Doc?' he said.

'Right oh,' I said. 'Bring Mrs Starkie over here and she can have a chat with my missis.'

The moment I'd said that, I knew I was in for trouble, but Celia wasn't the girl to let me down in public, however much she might towel me up in private, and Mrs Dicky was a good-natured little soul, so the French girl came over and took my chair.

'Well, old son, what's the trouble?' I asked, as soon as we were where the women couldn't hear us.

'My God, Doc, it's hell down in those cabins,' he said.

'Can't anything be done about it? You might work the oracle with the purser – he'd believe you.'

'What's wrong?' I asked, getting somewhat interested.

'You know where we are,' he said, 'on that damned lower deck?'

'Well, I'm sorry for you,' I said. 'I wouldn't like to be on that deck myself. It's bad enough where we are. But you aren't the only one, and you've got your wife there.'

At this he gave one loud laugh, which quite put the wind up me, for I thought Starkie was going off his head.

'And who else's wife?' he said, laughing again in this disagreeable way.

Seeing I looked a bit puzzled, he said I had better come down and see for myself. So down we went to the lower deck, D deck, where, as I think I told you, there were officers' cabins all along the starboard side. They were the same cabins that Larry, the dirty dog, had tried to pass off on me and Celia, three-berth cabins, with three wives together in one, and three husbands together in the other. It seemed a bit hard, but there are ways of arranging these things, for our men are resourceful birds. So I didn't see why Starkie should be rattled. He took me to an alleyway with a cabin on each side, and knocked at both doors. No one answered.

'All right, I'll show you,' he said.

The first cabin had three bunks. Two were made up, but I noticed the third one, which was really a couch under the porthole, had no bedding.

'Plenty of room for three,' I said.

'And more for two,' said Starkie, and laughed again.

'Bromide's what you want,' I said. 'There's nothing wrong here, anyway.'

Starkie opened the door of the opposite cabin. There were two bunks one above the other against the wall.

The couch under the porthole was made up as a berth, and right up against it was a kind of bed made with a mattress laid on cabin trunks. A blanket was hung down the middle to separate the two sets of berths, and you could hardly turn around, let alone open a cupboard or get at the washstand.

Then Starkie began to explain, and I don't know that I've ever laughed so much in my life. It seems that as soon as the sea went down and we got into the Mediterranean, all the husbands and wives on D deck held an indignation meeting. There they were, shut up like a harem or a monkery, and they didn't think it was a fair deal. It was like the old riddle of the fox and the goose and the bag of corn, three wives in one cabin and three husbands in another. They weren't all each other's husbands and wives either, which made matters worse, some being unmarried men, and a few civilians like Mrs Dicky and Miss Johnson. They went to the purser, but he hadn't a word to say, blaming it all on Horseferry Road. So they had a meeting in the saloon one day and made a kind of committee for D deck. The husbands each drew a poker hand and the winner got the cabin for himself and the missis for a week. The other four went over into the opposite cabin, taking a spare mattress with them, and dossed down as best they could, while the unmarried ones, men and ladies, sorted themselves out separately. Opinion was divided as to whether the two berths against the wall, or the couch with the trunks for a twin bed was the better bargain. There were serious drawbacks to both. Every week they changed round in turn.

'And where do you sleep?' I asked Starkie.

'My wife has the couch,' said Starkie, 'and I have to sleep on the trunks.'

He was nearly crying, and when I looked at the bed

of cabin trunks, and then looked at poor old Starkie with those tooth marks on his skinny neck, I laughed till I nearly cried myself. Whenever I looked at that poor chap afterwards, it was all I could do not to laugh.

'And what does Madam say?' I asked.

'She makes me turn in early,' said Starkie, blushing like a girl, 'and she won't let the others in till eleven. They don't mind. Say, Doc, have a heart. Can't you do anything?'

'Sorry, old son,' I said, 'but I'm not the purser. If you get chicken pox or measles, I can send you to hospital, otherwise you'll have to stay where you are. All I can do is to give Madam a sleeping draught.'

Well, it looked as if the poor little blighter would burst into tears, but I couldn't do anything, so I took him up again, and on the way I asked how they fixed things for the Captain's inspection. He said they had all put into a pool to bribe the steward and he got everything shipshape for the Captain's rounds, and afterwards he made up the beds as I had seen them, and hung up the blankets. The steward must have made about fifty pounds out of those poor couples.

'Well,' I said, 'when the ship does get on fire or strikes a reef, there will be some strange sights to be seen on D deck.'

When I got back to the boat deck, Madam and Celia were taking a walk up and down. I asked Mrs Dicky if she knew anything about the cabins on D deck, where she slept. Mrs Dicky was one of those women that don't need telling anything twice.

'What D deck knows it keeps to itself,' she said. 'I have no troubles. I share my cabin with Miss Johnson and some woman who is going out to Australia to be married, and we go to bed early and see and hear nothing, and I'd advise you to do the same, Major Bowen.'

'That's all right,' I said, 'it won't go any further, but I thought I'd let you know I'm in the secret.'

Upon this she took one look at poor Starkie, leaning miserably over the rail, and we both laughed till the cows came home.

This arrangement, I may now say, lasted the whole way out, and I don't believe the Old Man ever knew. If he did, he turned a blind eye, and that was the best and wisest thing he could do. Poor old Starkie must often have wished he had let well alone. Not that I let the cat out of the bag, but it somehow got round the ship, and someone would be sure to start whistling 'Mademoiselle from Armentiers' and Starkie would get wild.

The other French wife was quite a different sort from Madam Starkie, a nice quiet girl. She was going to have a kid – I mean you didn't need to be a doctor to see that – and looked pretty rotten. I did what I could for her, and thank the Lord she held out till we got to Sydney. A confinement on that ship would have been the last straw. Her husband was a Lieutenant Stanley, promoted from sergeant in France, and an absolutely dependable fellow in every way. He was one of our little gang of oldtimers and pulled his weight every time.

I forgot to mention another family that came on board at Port Said, an English naval officer called Pryce-Hughes, with his wife and kiddies. He was a decent fellow, going out to take a gunnery school at Flinders for two years. She was a Brisbane girl he had married when he was out there before, and a poisonous piece of work. It's funny the way our girls get their heads turned when they marry English naval men. Some of the nicest girls I have known have been completely spoiled that way. They seem to think they are too good for this world when they've got a sailor husband. This one was no exception. She was a pretty little woman, but she spoilt it all by the way she went on. She had two dear little kiddies, but she kept the poor little things in their perambulator on deck most of the day, so that they wouldn't play with the other kiddies, and only let them loose to play in the cabin. I was sorry for Pryce-Hughes, not to be able to stop his wife from making a fool of herself before the whole ship, but she had all the money and let him know it. She had a try for Smith, the Indian army man too, but got severely snubbed, much to the pleasure of all.

When we got past Suez the awnings were put up, and a sports committee was elected. Jack Howe was president, Mrs Dicky secretary, and Celia treasurer and they fairly made things hum. The Old Man allowed some of the lifeboats to be slung outside instead of on deck, so we got a little more room for games. I saw very little of Celia those days, as she was always running round chasing people to play off their rounds. I couldn't play regularly, but I came up when I could, just to please her. Of all the damn fool things in this world, chucking little bags of sand into a bucket is the one that appeals to me least, or throwing quoits. Deck tennis is more of a game, and I was pretty good at that, having won the mixed finals with Mrs Howe. Mrs Henley wouldn't play. She gave a good subscription, but she got her chair pulled into a corner where she wouldn't be in the way, and sat there all day with Smith. They were often there up till last thing at night, he always talking away and she not saying very much.

It got warmer every day, which suited me down to the ground. The men mostly went about on their own decks stripped to the waist or just a singlet, and the whole place smelt like a cheap Turkish bath. It was about this time that I had a very disagreeable experience. Mrs Pryce-Hughes had somehow discovered that my Mater's people were what she called of good family. It is true that the Mallards were connexions of the earl of that name, but they never made a song about it. Also the present earl was a real rip, who ran through several fortunes and was divorced by two wives, and they didn't wish to encourage him. They had had enough trouble when he came out to Sydney as an A.D.C. and nearly married one of the richest girls in Woollahra, only her family discovered just in time that he was keeping two little establishments in different parts of the city and kicked him out. The dirty part of it was that he cleared out without doing anything for these two other girls, and I hear the language those Janes used was worth hearing.

So this dame thought I was good enough for her, but she took no trouble to be nice to Celia, and that is what I won't stand for. She had asked me once or twice to have drinks in her cabin, but I always made an excuse. If she wanted me, she could ask my wife.

One morning I was down in the D deck surgery when she came in. I was surprised, because there was a surgery for the saloon deck, but she hadn't come for medicine. She said she wanted to see the men's quarters. I wasn't at all keen, and I told her that Colonel Picking was the man to ask. She talked a lot of bunk about Picking not being quite our sort, and how she would feel safer with me. What the devil she wanted to do there at all, you can search me, but some women are born fools. Anyway there was the orderly grinning, and Higgins, who had come in with a message, looking at me to see how I'd get out of it, but nothing would stop her. So very much against my will I took her down the alleyway and showed her one or two cabins. The diggers were in some of them, smoking or playing cards on their bunks, and they didn't get up and salute or do any tricks. I felt all kinds of a fool. The digger has a great pride of his own and much resents any kind of interference or condescension. I knew quite well what those fellows would be saying about Mrs Pryce-Hughes, and though she thoroughly deserved it, I was annoyed that they should get such a bad opinion of a naval man's wife.

We passed the galley and went out on to the well deck. Mrs Pryce-Hughes admired the washing hanging out, and she admired the two-up school, and I felt more of a fool than ever. She had on a pretty summer frock, some kind of a pink musliny affair it was, all fluffy and billowing, and a big pink hat, and I don't deny that she looked very pretty. She got up on the grating over the cargo hatch and stood there, admiring everything, while I wished her husband would come and fetch her. The diggers were passing all kinds of remarks in a kind of aside, and I could only pray she wouldn't hear them. Anyway if she had she probably wouldn't have understood them. I hope not.

Little Higgins, who understood me very well, had been hanging about, I didn't know why, and presently he came up and saluted.

'Excuse me, sir,' he said, 'I think the lady had better come off the hatch.'

'Oh, must I, Sergeant?' said that fool woman. 'Am I breaking the rules?'

'Not at all, madam,' said Higgins, 'but the troops on E deck, if you'll excuse me mentioning it, have passed the word round that there's something to see.'

I jumped on the grating. About twenty diggers were standing just below that fool woman, looking up and laughing and joking very freely. Whether they did it on purpose I shall never know, or whether Higgins was bluffing, but Mrs Pryce-Hughes gave one hoot and jumped off the grating and streaked up the ladder on to the promenade deck. There was a coolness between me and her after that, but I won seven quid off her husband at poker before we got to Colombo.

It was pretty hot in the Red Sea, but nothing to what I have experienced. Going back to Australia after Gallipoli – I was at Mena House hospital with enteric and was sent home for a spell – we had a following breeze, and the Old Man had to stop sometimes to let us get a breath of air. I have heard of ships that had to go backwards to get cool, but seeing is believing, as they say. Two stokers died on that trip, poor chaps. We didn't lose any this trip, but when I saw them come up for a spell, after their shifts, all black and sweaty, with their faces where they had rubbed them dead white, I felt there was much to be said against a stoker's life. The elder kids all stood the heat wonderfully, but the babies began to look a bit peaky. Do what you may, you cannot keep babies properly fit on a long voyage. None of them were ill, but the poor little beggars got a bit off colour and didn't seem as keen on their bottles as they used to be. I worked away like anything trying to please them, and giving them drinks of orange juice, but we were very short of fruit. However, we reckoned to get plenty more on at Colombo.

From Suez to Colombo we had perfect weather all the way, and life fell into a sort of routine. After breakfast I had my surgery work, which now fell entirely on Colonel Bird and myself, as Lyon was more or less confined to his cabin after Suez, which was where he had his row with the old doctor. What with the babies and the diggers, this took me till nearly midday. There was plenty of grousing among the men, and the discipline was still very slack, but the idea that every day was bringing them nearer home seemed to cheer everyone up, and tempers were fairly good. I saw Cavanagh about far too often for

my liking, but so long as he didn't give any trouble, I
didn't see the sense in making any. He often saluted me.
We had a kind of understanding of each other ever since
the day I had set his thumb.

After work I'd have a yarn and a drink in the smoke-
room, or down with old Schultz, who was a great old
fellow, or play some deck tennis. After lunch everyone
who wasn't on duty would have a kind of lay-down.
There were sometimes some more surgery cases after tea,
or I'd fossick round with Jerry and Jack Howe, picking
up the news. I never belonged to the poker school,
though I like a game occasionally. Those fellows played
morning, noon and night. Most of them weren't married
and I never got to know them all. There they would sit
all day, shirts open to the waist, sleeves rolled up, shorts
or khaki slacks, and deck shoes. Never mind how hot it
was, they were as happy as Larry. Celia and I would
often get a game of bridge after dinner, if we could we
got Jack Howe and Mrs Dicky to join us. Mrs Howe
didn't play bridge, but she had the finest poker sense
I've ever known in a woman, or in most men, with a
face that gave nothing away. It was her poker sense that
got Mrs Dicky out of a difficulty after Colombo. She and
Jack were having trouble below, because their cabin had,
as I think I said, no ventilation except into the alleyway,
and they had an electric fan that wouldn't work. So they
took their mattresses out in the little alleyway between
the cabins and slept there. Catchpole made a bit of a
fuss, but ten bob soon settled that.

It was here that we had all the trouble with the wind-
shoots. As soon as we got past Suez, I told Catchpole to
put ours in our port. He accordingly did so, and also put
one in the port at the end of our alleyway, so that if we
hooked the door back at night, we got quite a nice
draught, besides the electric fan. Two days out from

Suez the alleyway wind-shoot had gone. I roared Catchpole up, but he said it wasn't his fault. Then one went from the cabin across the way, and one afternoon I found mine gone. Of course I raised hell, and next day it came back, only to vanish again that afternoon. But I had scratched my name on it, so I gave Catchpole five bob, and told him to find it. Sure enough he did find it, down on D deck, in one of the three-berth cabins. Of course the trouble was there weren't enough to go round – there just wouldn't have been on a ship like that. It was the D deck steward who had pinched it and several others from our deck. I got Catchpole to get the D deck steward, and I talked to him like a Dutch uncle. It turned out the diggers had been pinching the D deck wind-shoots, so the D deck steward had been pinching ours.

'All right,' I said, 'this funny game will now stop. Pinch what you like, but the next time my wind-shoot, or the one from the alleyway is borrowed, I'll do my damnedest as ship's doctor, and everyone will wish they had left little Willie alone. You can pass the word round to the boys.'

After that I had no more trouble myself, but what went on in the other cabins was like hunt-the-slipper. The C. of E. padre, the Reverend Brown, was on our deck, and here his wife surprised us all by showing great determination. It turned out she had been all over the place doing missionary work with her husband, and had that pleasing feeling that all others but herself and family were not worth troubling about, except if they needed converting. She froze on to her wind-shoot like a bulldog. One day I was down there, and I saw the D deck steward sneak into her cabin. A minute later he came out with a wind-shoot. I was going to jump on him, but he went into the cabin opposite, where the padre's kids slept. Hardly had he gone in, when there was a most almighty noise. I went to see who was being murdered, but it was only Mrs Brown, who had been laying for that steward all that afternoon. She had taken the wind-shoot away from him and was banging his head against the corner of the washstand. The door was hooked open, so I could hear it all through the curtain. She gave him a sermon, just for all the world as if he was one of her natives, and from that day he never came near her cabin. He go it both ways, because Catchpole half killed him for coming up again on his deck. But after that the Bowen and Brown families had all the wind-shoots they wanted.

6

Andy gets his Bluff called

The sports committee were running a fancy-dress dance
two nights before we were due at Colombo. There was to
be a parade and prizes, and the following night the
diggers were to have their dance on the starboard deck,
to which ladies from the first class were invited, it
standing to reason that there were enough men already.
I always think a fancy-dress ball is a fool affair, but it
pleased Celia. Old Colonel Bird wanted to go as some
kind of a monk, so I said all right, I'd be on duty that
night, and very pleased I was not to be mixed up in it.
The committee wanted a fancy-dress dinner first, but
didn't get much support, so dinner was put half an hour
earlier, to give people time to dress.

I haven't mentioned before that Mrs Jerry had been
having trouble with her nurse. She was quite agreeable
to calling the girl Gladys, but she wasn't agreeable to the
way Gladys was making friends among the officers. Not
that she was a wowser, nor did she not want the girl to
have a good time; but after all she was the kiddies'
nurse, and Mrs Jerry wasn't paying her to sit round with
the officers.

'That's always the way with English girls,' said Mrs
Jerry when I went in to ask for some earrings she had
promised to lend Celia. She was bathing the kids, and
her temper was right up the pole.

'You sit down, Tom,' she said, 'and dry these kids

while I find the earrings. I've given that girl of mine some scarves and things to dress up in, and what do you think she has done?'

I didn't know, so I didn't say anything. There were times when it was safer not to.

'She always goes to the first dinner,' said Mrs Jerry. 'So, if you please, she comes back here, dresses while I'm at my dinner, and walks out on me, leaving me to put the children to bed. I don't know where she is. Probably on the boat deck with the second officer who is her latest. Oh, my God,' said Mrs Jerry, sitting down and putting young Dick's pyjamas on, 'I always said I'd never have an English girl again and I wish I'd stuck to it. There isn't one in a thousand that doesn't get her head turned on the voyage. They all get to think they're as good as their employers, and when they get to Australia and find they aren't one of the family, it's tears and sulks and wanting to go home. I've been had that way before, and I'm a fool to be had again. She's a good girl, but if she goes on cutting a bit off her sleeves and the neck of her frocks every day, she will be left in her chemise, and then where shall we be?'

Of course this made the kids laugh, and we had a fine chase around the cabin. Then we tucked them up and I took the earrings. I asked Mrs Jerry if I could do anything for her, but she said no, she could manage all right.

'But mind, Tom,' she said, 'don't you let Celia have an English girl. You have to find friends for them, and they don't get on with them, and they don't understand doing a lot of different jobs. Give me an Australian girl every time. They may be a bit rough, but they are great workers, and they don't mind what they do, because they've seen their mother do it all, and they know that I can do it all and better than they can. My girl I had

103

in Adelaide was a treasure, but she wasn't the only one like that. It's true I gave her thirty-five shillings a week, but she'd cook, and do the whole house, and most of the washing, and take the children any time, and answer the telephone sensibly, and make lovely cakes. The only thing she wouldn't do was wait at table, because she was shy of company, but I was just getting her trained when this war had to come along. And don't stand there wasting my time,' said Mrs Jerry, 'because I've got to get Jerry and myself dressed, and it's a surprise.' So she pushed me out of the cabin.

Celia was in some sort of gypsy get-up, with Mrs Jerry's earrings and her pretty hair in plaits, the way she wears it in bed. She is a bonzer kid – I don't know when I've seen anyone to touch her. Whatever the committee may have thought, my little missis was the prettiest thing on the boat that night or any other night for that matter.

There was a ship's band of sorts which was to play, so when I heard them starting, I went along to the smoke-room and had a yarn with Stone about the boxing competition we were getting up. He had some good navy champions, and we could put in some good fighters, so we reckoned we would get a good display. The A.I.F. officers were putting up a purse, and the fight was to come off after we left Colombo. Stone wasn't dancing, and it was just as well, for he had already had as much as was good for him. Presently Anstruther came in.

'Come on, Major, and see the parade,' he said. 'It's a fine show, and Mrs Bowen looks lovely. We'll bring old Stone along with us.'

'Not on your life,' I said.

'But he's one of the judges,' said Anstruther.

However, Stone was by now half asleep on a seat, so we judged it best to leave him with Tim the barman, a hard case if ever there was one, though he never touched a drop himself.

'Who are the other judges?' I said.

'Colonel Picking and Mrs Picking and Miss Johnson and Major Barrett.'

This Major Barrett was the staff major whose cabin I had pinched. He was a nice old bird, but his wife was a terror. However, I never had much to do with them.

Well, we got along the deck and watched the parade. Of course there was no question that Celia was far the prettiest, but there were some good costumes. Mrs Pryce-Hughes had some kind of an Eastern outfit with a veil, and she had bare feet and had put rouge on her toes. I suppose the idea was henna, but it wasn't a success. Jack Howe and his missis were Merry Peasants. Mrs Dicky came as a Chinese coolie and looked very attractive, though hardly the figure for the part. Old Colonel Bird had put on a big black beard and a sort of robe and looked for all the world like one of the French priests. Indeed trouble was caused by people mistaking them all for each other, and the priests went to Captain Spooner to complain, but he sent them to blazes. Captain Smith had an Indian get-up with a turban, but he didn't parade. He wanted to dance with Mrs Henley who was in a green evening dress with a mask, but not dressed up. The success of the evening were Jerry and Mrs Jerry as Dad and Mum, with two or three young officers as Joe and the rest of the family out of 'On Our Selection'. Where Jerry had raised the togs he wore, you can search me, but I suppose he got the diggers to contribute. He had got some false whiskers and a filthy old pair of slacks all patched, and a seedy old coat and a real cocky farmer's hat, all greasy with a broken brim. Mrs Jerry had a black skirt and an apron and a blouse with checks and a kind of bonnet. Joe and the others were champion too, and they all had the real back-block drawl, till we all got quite homesick. It was donkey's years since I'd heard the word 'cow' said the way those boys said it – 'keaow' is the nearest I can get, but you can't make it long enough in print. Everyone clapped like mad, and we all thought they'd get the prize. But the judges said it was difficult to decide, and would they all go around again. There were to be prizes for the most artistic lady's and gentleman's costume and for the best comics.

So the band struck up and the procession began again. By now Smith and Mrs Henley were dancing on the little bit of landing at the top of the companion way, just outside the lounge, looking as if they were drugged, not seeing anyone. It gave me the creeps to look at them. It wasn't somehow natural. When the parade came round again, there were some fresh faces I hadn't seen before. Anstruther was a toreador and looked quite the lady-killer with little sideboards. Anderson was got up as some sort of Dago and by God it suited him. You'd have said he had got into his own skin. I saw Mrs Jerry's nurse rigged out as a fairy queen or something of the sort. But I didn't take much notice of her costume, because near the tail of the procession came the handsomest girl I'd ever seen. We all stared at her. No one could place her, and it was supposed that she got on at Port Said and had been in her cabin all the time. It is extraordinary the way you can be on a full boat for days and not know who is there. She was fairly tall, a lovely figure, and moved as gracefully as a swan. She had a low-necked frock and a rope of pearls, and wore a wreath on her golden hair. I know it sounds like the Christmas panto-mime, but there she was. And a lovely skin too, all pink and white. She didn't look at anyone, but moved round with her fine big eyes on the ground. The band stopped, the judges began to consult, and we all buzzed round

106

wondering who the girl was. She must have gone back to her cabin for something, as she was not to be seen just then.

Major Barrett told me later in the smoke-room that there was some unpleasantness about giving the prizes. He and Picking plumped for the strange girl as the most artistic, straight away, and for Jerry and his missis for the best comics, and Colonel Bird as the most artistic man. Mrs Picking wanted Celia for best lady, Anderson for best man, and the Fairchilds for best comics. Miss Johnson wanted Mrs Howe for best lady, Anderson for best man, and a couple from D deck who came as the Ugly Sisters for best comic. Of course the Fairchilds were miles and away the funniest, but ever since the row about the baths Miss Johnson had been sharpening her claws for Mrs Jerry, and also for Celia because she was my wife and I had been in the bath affair – though what I could have done I don't know, for you must answer a lady when she speaks to you, and I couldn't say the kiddies were mine when they weren't. Neither of the ladies would so much as hear of the strange girl being suggested for a prize, and neither of the men were going to let that little squirt Anderson get away with it. So there they were. If old Stone had been more sober it would have been all right, as he could have given a casting vote. The time was passing, and the crowd was getting impatient, so they asked the Old Man, who was giving away the prizes, to give his views. He hadn't seen all the show, so they had to have the parade once more. They were all getting a bit sick of it, and Colonel Bird's beard was coming off. The strange girl slipped in again at the rear of the procession. The Old Man's eyes fairly goggled when he saw her. It didn't take him long to make up his mind, and the results were, the strange girl most artistic lady, old Doctor Bird most artistic man (for

the Old Man hadn't any use for Anderson), and the
Fairchilds best comic. This seemed to me quite just. Celia
was of course by far the prettiest girl on board, but this
other girl made a wonderful effect, and there is no doubt
she had great style.

All this time the gramophone had been going at the
head of the companion way, and Mrs Henley and Smith
had been dancing in those few square feet like dumb
lunatics. They looked very well together and would have
had a good chance of a prize, but they were standoffish
and wouldn't take part in the fun. There are many times
when I feel quite a want of sympathy for those I am
among, but I always do my best to make things cheery.
I always feel it is up to one to do this.

Mrs Dicky, who was secretary, went to ask the strange
girl her name, but couldn't find her, and when the prizes
came to be given out, she was still nowhere to be found.
All the men had a good look, but she had disappeared
and the ladies said it was a pity to go on waiting, so the
Old Man said the prize for the best woman should go
to Mrs Dicky as the other lady hadn't claimed it. Mrs
Dicky was very popular, so no one objected, not even
Miss Johnson.

When the ladies had gone to bed, a crowd of us were
in the smoke-room, having a hand of poker, when Nancy
walked in. He was still in his Dago's get-up and looked
pretty pleased with himself.

'You missed the fun,' said Jack Howe. 'Why didn't you
come and help us look for that pretty girl.'

'Perhaps I didn't need to,' said Nancy.

We all began to take an interest.

'What do you know about her?' asked Jack.

'Ask the moon,' said Anderson, with such an expression
that I could have kicked his pants. He didn't need
pressing, and he told us the tale how he had been up on

108

the boat deck with that lovely girl and what a little Don Juan he had been.

'Oh, cut it out, Anderson,' said Hobson, who was a promoted sergeant. He had been in Palestine with Allenby in the Light Horse. 'You haven't the guts to kiss a pretty girl.'

Anderson looked nasty, but he said nothing, he just pulled a pink garter out of his pocket and held it up for us to look at, and put it away again.

I am very broadminded myself in many ways, but I have never liked to hear a man speak disrespectfully of a lady in public. It is a great privilege to get the love of a real good woman such as I have, and gives me a very chivalrous feeling about other women. I threw my hand in – a full house it was too – and said it was time for decent fellows to be in bed. All followed my example and Nancy was left alone with Tim. He wouldn't cut any ice with Tim, who was known to have been married in Sydney and Perth, and found the War a great relief as the strain of keeping two families going was too much for him in every way.

Next day the whole ship was buzzing about the girl. No one had seen her again. All the cabin stewards and the stewardesses had been questioned, but could tell nothing, or wouldn't. Surgery was heavy that day owing to a free fight between some Irish. They had given and received a fair number of black eyes, damaged shins, etc. I got Father Glennie down, and he read the Riot Act to his lot, while I towelled up the Orangemen. We settled to let them have it out at a boxing competition later.

One of the R.C. fellows called Casey had a cut on his neck.

'Easy with the bandages, Doc,' he said. 'I've got to look my best for the dance tonight.'

'If you weren't a youngster,' I said, 'I'd shove you into hospital to teach you sense. What the devil does it matter to you what a man's religion is?'

'It's not that, Doctor,' said the boy, he was quite a kid, 'but the dirty Protestants had it over us that the old doctor went to the ball as a holy father, so one way and another there was trouble.'

At that Father Glennie sailed into him, and I ticked off the C. of E. chaps who had started the argument, and I strapped up Casey's cut. It was at the back and wouldn't show much.

'Now keep your fists to yourself, Casey,' I said, 'and I'll promise you a real good fight before we get to Fremantle.'

He was delighted, and shook hands and went away grinning from ear to ear.

That afternoon young Dick had to fall off something on the boat deck – I wasn't there when he had the fall, but the kid was always climbing somewhere he had no call to be – and was a bit sick. Only very mild concussion, and he was as fit as a fiddle in a couple of days. But Mrs Jerry got the wind well and truly up about him, and spent the evening in the cabin, which was why she missed all the fun. We were due at Colombo early next morning and everyone feels restless the last night before a landfall. There was something going on below too, but I couldn't yet find out what. However, I had my spies out, Higgins and one or two others, and I thought I'd probably get a line on any mischief that was about. Mrs Henley and Smith were sitting together on the boat deck all day. He was doing all the talking as usual, and she said hardly anything. I said that the night before they were dancing together in that doped sort of way. Well, I didn't mention it at the time, but I had thought more than once that he was a dope-bug. You know the look they have. But I hardly knew the fellow, and what with my work, and worrying about the men below, and trying not to let on to Celia that there was anything to worry about, I hadn't any time to spare for Smith. And I couldn't have done anything if I had. I didn't want Celia to get scared about things, though Lord knows there was plenty to get scared about. I am a reserved kind of chap in many ways, but I have very deep feelings and one of them is a very deep appreciation of my little missis. She is everything to me, and she has been a real little pal all through.

The diggers' dance was timed for eight o'clock. In view of conditions below Colonel Picking had an idea of stopping it, thinking the men might be inclined to be a bit obstreperous, but he was persuaded not to do such a damn silly thing. The digger may be a bit rough, but where women are concerned he is a real gentleman at heart, and I knew the boys wouldn't let us down that evening if the officers' wives went to the dance. Higgins told me their committee had made a raid on the men's cabins and confiscated any beer they found till after the dance. The diggers grumbled a bit, but agreed they ought to put up a good show for the ladies, so I did not anticipate much trouble.

The officers mostly were in the smoke-room that evening, as they weren't wanted at the dance. We had a men's bridge tournament going on, and a whist drive, and there was the usual poker school, and some N.C.O.'s who had got commissions were playing euchre, and you couldn't get a pin between the tables. I was playing bridge that night, so I missed the beginning of the fun, but Celia who was there from the jump told me the parts I missed. The diggers had a wonderful evening arranged, with artistic hand-painted programmes and refreshments. We had some fine artists among the men, several of whom had contributed to various A.I.F. papers,

and some were real painters in civil life, doing carica-
tures and landscapes, etc., with no difficulty. The dances
were waltzes, foxtrots, the Valeta and the Circassian
circle. The Valeta is a pretty and graceful dance, though
not much known out of non-commissioned circles. The
officers' wives were very keen to learn, and the diggers
enjoyed teaching them. It is a bit like the Barn Dance
and a bit like the Washington Post, and a bit like a
waltz, and when well danced is very effective. The only
snag was the heat of the evening, which caused the
diggers to be a bit damp. Some were dancing in their
tunics and some in their shirts, but the general effect was
the same, and it was a messy one. Celia said she couldn't
do otherwise than be pleased when she saw Miss Johnson
in a pea-green frock with the back all smeared with the
marks where her partner's strong and perspiring arm
had been round her. You would say those diggers had
never sweated before, the way they came off on everything that night. Celia, who is a sensible kid, had on a
sort of silk affair that could be washed and a pair of
white silk gloves she happened to have with her, otherwise her frock would have been in a similar case to that
of Miss Johnson. I must say that the idea of that old
tabby dressing up in a pea-green frock and getting it
spoilt by the licentious soldiery appealed greatly to my
sense of humour.

Mrs Jerry's nurse was there, looking very smart with
some rouge she had borrowed from Mrs Dicky. She
would only dance with sergeants and corporals. This was
all right as long as they had their tunics on, but when
they appeared in their shirt-sleeves she was a bit at a
loss. One of the diggers, a greasy young Wop called
Alameda, who the boys called Macaroni by way of fun,
kidded her he was an N.C.O. and got three dances. But
though much upset when his cobbers gave the show

112

away, she forgave him because he was an Italian. As a matter of fact, he wasn't, because all the Wops in Melbourne where he came from are Sicilians. His people had the Alameda Fruit Palace somewhere in St Kilda and were quite well off.

Well, about ten o'clock the diggers sent word into the smoke-room they hoped Mr Anderson would come and see the dance, and judge which was the best couple in the Valeta. Nancy had been losing steadily at poker, so he was quite pleased for an excuse to get out. Hardly was he gone when my surgery orderly came to the door and stood looking for me. Thinking there was a casualty below I went to the door. He said the committee sent an invitation to all officers to go round to the other end of the starboard deck, as there was a surprise for them. Some of the officers thought it a bit too free, but on the whole we decided to go. Colonel Picking and Major Barrett with a couple more stayed behind, which was just as well, as old Picking would have passed out if he had seen what happened.

A whole crowd of us went aft, some to the end of the deck, and some to the door just outside the lounge which opened on to the starboard side, of which I was one. The band were striking up for the Valeta, when who should come up the deck but the strange girl. My word, she was a beaut. She was dressed just like the night before, with a kind of shining scarf affair round her neck. All the diggers got quite quiet suddenly as she came up within a few feet of where I was standing and turned to Anderson who was leaning against the rail.

'Oh, you naughty man,' she said, and her voice was a kind of a shock, for it was not a pretty one and not quite refined, 'where is my garter?'

If Anderson felt as silly as he looked, he must have felt pretty silly.

'Let me see if it's in your pocket, dear,' said the girl.

She lifted her arms, lovely white arms they were too, and went for Anderson but he ducked and ran over to us, quite pale and upset.

'Oh, Tom, do do something,' said Celia, grabbing at me. But I told her to be quiet for a moment. The girl turned round, facing all us officers and said in a quite different voice:

'Have I won the stakes, boys?'

And she took off her golden hair and someone gave her a cigarette. Of course I had seen the piece of strapping on her neck when she lifted her arms, and the scarf fell off a bit, so I had tumbled to it, but I wasn't going to give the show away. When Casey took his golden wig off, there was such a noise that they might have heard us at Colombo. He had been a female impersonator in a famous concert party in France, and I've never seen a better get-up. Hair, eyes, figure, hands, feet, he would have deceived anyone. There was only the voice that gave one a bit of a shock, but after all a pretty girl sometimes has a quite common voice.

If Anderson hadn't been such a conceited little runt, we would have been sorry for him, but there was hardly a soul on board who had a good word for him. He pushed through and made for his cabin. We were all laughing till we were nearly sick, and what made it all the funnier was that the women couldn't understand what had happened. No one let out to them about Andy's behaviour in the smoke-room the previous night, so they hadn't an idea what the joke was. Every married man had to turn in early that night and tell his missis all about it.

It was about at this time that Casey took off his stockings, saying he couldn't keep them up without the garter Captain Anderson had stolen, and began to imitate

a dancing girl in Cairo, at which point we very regret-
fully took the ladies into the lounge and passed the word
to Casey to continue his performance further forward.
It was the first time I'd wished I wasn't married, and you
can take it that the other married officers shared my
regrets.

Of course a lot of them said they had spotted Casey
from the jump, but weren't giving him away. Well, the
Lord loves a cheerful liar. I just looked into the smoke-
room before turning in.

'Did everything go off all right, Doctor?' asked old
Picking.

'First rate, sir,' I said. 'Captain Anderson was the life
of the party.'

Those who were not on deck said they would have
given a month's pay not to have missed Andy's face. In
an ordinary way the whole ship would have talked of
nothing else for a week, but on the following day we
came to Colombo, and there we had our troubles which
completely made us forget Nancy's.

7

The Digger isn't a bad Chap

Next morning we woke up to find ourselves at Colombo. It was a bonzer day, and all were looking forward to getting on shore and having a decent meal for once, and perhaps a real bed. For ship's food is not the same as shore food, and after going through the galley several times you lose your relish for some things. However, what doesn't sicken will fatten, and if the cooks wouldn't wear their white caps in the hot weather, it is hardly to be surprised at. Considering there was no refrigerating plant we had done pretty well, and there was very little suspicion of a taint about the meat. We were to get a lot of fresh stuff on at Colombo, fruit and so forth, and I was looking forward to giving my babies a treat.

The notice was posted up after breakfast that shore leave would be given to all officers except such as were on the roster for duty. The diggers were to take it in turn to go on shore, always leaving a sufficient guard for the prisoners. Most of the men had been to Colombo before, and looked forward to a happy time in the bazaars. Ever since the row about the wind-shoots Celia had chummed up with the Reverend Brown and his wife, and they had asked us to join them. It seemed he had been a missionary there for some time, and they both knew the lingo and said they could help us to do our shopping cheap. I wanted to go out to the Galle Face for the night, but the padre had to stay at the G.O.H.

because he was expecting some of his old pals and pupils. Mrs Jerry wouldn't leave young Dick, who was still a bit under the weather, and Jerry was on duty. Jerry said he didn't care anyway if he never saw another nigger again. So I and Celia, and the Browns with their three kids, and the Howes, arranged to do some sightseeing together.

Before we went on shore Higgins asked if he could see me. I had him in my cabin, because old Bird was in the surgery. He had offered to stay on the ship so I could take Celia on shore, a kindness which was much appreciated by us. He also shared Jerry's views about niggers.

'I thought I'd better let you know, sir,' said Higgins, 'that the prisoners are all going on shore.'

'The hell they are,' I said. 'Does the Colonel know?'

'I don't know, sir,' said Higgins, 'but I wouldn't trouble him, sir. He can't stop them, so he'd better not know anything about it.'

'Well, this isn't my pigeon,' I said, 'I'm only a doctor. But I would like to know a bit more about what is happening.'

So Higgins told me a long story. It seems the prisoners had been making such nasty remarks about what they would do to the guard when they got out, that the guard had told them they could go to hell their own way. There had been quite a little turn-up about it the night before, after the dance, the prisoners saying they'd chuck the ——— guard overboard the first chance they got, the guard arguing that having survived Gallipoli and France, they were not now seeking a watery grave. Hence the guards unlocked the cells, and Cavanagh and his pals promptly chucked the keys into the Indian Ocean. There hadn't been any trouble yet. The jailbirds were as pleased as Larry to be out again, and after borrowing some

cigarettes and things from the nearest cabins, they just
sat as meek as curates till the leave boats began to go on
shore, upon which they stoushed one or two that tried
to interfere, and went happily off to the pier.

I rang for Catchpole and told him to find Jerry, and
got Higgins to run over the main facts again. We came
to the conclusion, after nutting things out, that there
would probably be a good deal more trouble on shore
than on the ship. Jerry said he'd do his best to stiffen old
Picking up, and he told me to keep in touch with Howe
and Hobson, and one or two more of the decent chaps,
and stand by for trouble after dark.

'They'll be all right today,' he said, 'mooching round
the bazaars and filling up with bad drink, but after
sunset things may brighten up a bit, and the Major won't
be any good.'

'My oath, he won't,' I said, for Barrett, though a decent
little chap, was the last man to handle a difficult situation.

So we dismissed Higgins, and Mrs Jerry gave us a list
of shopping as long as your arm to do for her.

Gosh, I can tell you it was good-oh to get ashore
again. Being February the weather was just right, and
it was nice to smell the old Eastern smell again. Our
party got rickshaws, and the padre took us round the
shops and the ladies did a wonderful amount of shopping.
The padre wouldn't stand any nonsense and the way he
beat those niggers down was a treat. Some of them
remembered him quite well. Those were good days, for
the rupee was as low as it has ever been. I've forgotten
exactly what we got for our English money, but in the
bazaars the diggers were getting as much as thirty-seven
shillings for English sovereigns, of which they had
managed to get a good many. Of course they had to
change it and lost on the exchange, and then they spent
it all, or had their pockets gone through by their lady

friends, but they had their fun while it lasted. While riding through the bazaars I saw Cavanagh bargaining for a monkey, and looking like Mother's Good Boy. He saw me and waved, and then he came running after me.

'See here, Doc,' he said, 'you done me a good turn with that bleeding Orangeman the time I bust me thumb, and I've never gone back on a pal yet. Where are you going tonight?'

'G.O.H.' I said, not that it was any business of his, but civility costs nothing.

'You take the missis to the Galle Face,' he said. 'Least said soonest mended, but you can —— well take me word that the —— hotel won't be healthy.'

'It isn't a doctor's business to mind about unhealthy places,' I said, 'but thanks for the office, old son.'

Cavanagh was a damned nuisance, and he had been in jail for nearly doing in a pal and his girl, who had been Cavanagh's girl but he had his points.

We all went out to Mount Lavinia and had lunch, and in the afternoon we bathed and the kiddies had a bonzer time. Celia and Mrs Howe were like kids themselves, all excited and pleased. They bought some lace and some tortoiseshell stuff and Mrs Brown did the bargaining. I told Jack about Cavanagh, and he agreed with me that if the men were going to pull any rough stuff we'd better be on hand. We all had dinner at the G.O.H. where Hobson joined us and Father Glennie, so we were a cheery party. Most of our lot had gone to the Galle Face where there was a smart dance that night, but I was pleased to see we could count on half a dozen good men, including ourselves. I reckoned if Jack and Hobson and I, with Father Glennie, couldn't keep things quiet, we weren't the old soldiers we ought to be.

The dinner was a cheery affair, and we all felt the worst part of our journey was over and Australia in sight, but had we known what was to come we should have known differently. After dinner the Browns went off to visit some Indian friends and the rest of us went into the lounge. There was some talk of dancing, but none of us felt very keen, so we just sat and yarned, and the usual touts came round selling jade and silk, and offering to take your cheque from Australia, but we weren't interested. They are as cunning as a cartload of monkeys, those natives, and regular swindlers. The Ghurkas are different. We had some of them with us in the Canal scrapping, jolly little chaps, keen as mustard. They were real white men and as clean as you or I. I got quite fond of one chap whose name I have forgotten, for we used to call him Kedgeree, and many's the yarn we had, him in his lingo, and I in English. But we understood each other wonderfully.

Stone came through the lounge and I asked where his men were. He told me they were all just going back to the ship, which was a considerable relief to my mind, because if there was to be any trouble and his men blew into it, the diggers would probably have killed half of them. Stone went off, and all was going peacefully, and we were just thinking of turning in, when there was a most unholy row from the street outside. I suppose the same thought came uppermost in all our minds: 'Damn those blasted fools', but owing to the presence of ladies no one expressed it. Celia and Mrs Howe looked a bit scared, but we told them to go to bed and not worry about us. Celia looked quite white, poor kid, but I knew she'd be all right in the hotel, unless the diggers took it into their heads to burn it down. But I reckoned if there was any burning to be done they'd start on the bazaars, for some of the men had been in Cairo and had experience. Jack, Hobson and I buckled our belts on and went out to see the fun.

120

It was a bonzer night with that sort of velvety sky and lots of stars. A crowd of our men, pretty tight, were coming along singing and shouting, holding up all the traffic. The hotel people were putting up shutters and closing the front door. The rickshaw men mostly took to their heels, leaving the rickshaws and the passengers stranded. The diggers were turning the passengers out, not too gently either, and taking each other for rides. You would have laughed to see fat old Cingalese birds being turned out of those rickshaws like a pudding out of a bowl, but it was geting beyond a laughing matter. Not content with riding up and down, some of the diggers made for a stand of rickshaws which were drawn up along the pavement, and knocked them over one after another like nine-pins. What with the crash of the breaking rickshaws and the boys yelling and singing, you couldn't hear yourself speak. They were having rickshaw races too, and a lot of money was being laid. I saw Cavanagh lean out of his rickshaw and grab at the man who was overtaking him. The wheels locked, and they fairly pulled each other out on to the road, and the whole affair came to the ground in a heap. The diggers' language did every justice to the situation.

The native police were hovering about, but they couldn't do much. I was afraid the military would be turned out, in which case our fellows would have gone right off the handle and gone for them bald-headed. If there is one thing the digger cannot bear it is being interfered with. I saw young Casey in the crowd, so I hauled him out by the slack of his pants. I had to shout into his ear to make him hear me. Luckily he wasn't so drunk as most of them.

'Where's the rest of the crowd?' I said.

'Beating up the bazaars, Doc,' he said, 'but don't you worry. You go to bed and we'll settle the —— niggers.'

'The hell you will,' I said, and then Father Glennie came up.

'Here's one of your lambs, Father,' I said. 'He's been drinking that muck in the bazaars and will probably be dead or blind tomorrow, but before he passes out, see if you can make out what's happening.'

Well, the father put the fear of purgatory into young Casey, and we made out from what he told us that the diggers had made a nuisance of themselves around the bazaars, but there hadn't been any rioting till they got down to the hotel, and then someone started the rickshaw game. The digger is like a kid. If he gets hold of a new game he will play with nothing else till he is sick of it. Three of us and a padre couldn't stop about fifty diggers upsetting rickshaws and smashing windows, and the worst of it was we had no idea how many more might be coming down from the bazaars at any moment. The most we could do was to shepherd them down to the quay and hope to get them off to the ship.

'You go round, Casey, and tell any of the boys that are sober to get the others down to the boats,' said Father Glennie, 'and next time you come to confession I may let you off a bit of your penance.'

Young Casey wasn't a bad kid, he was just doing what the others did. I could see Father Glennie had him scared, and that often has a wonderfully sobering effect. Casey and one or two more got through the crowd to the upper end of the street, and gradually the mob began to move down towards the pier. I can't tell you all that happened, because I was only in one place at a time, which was down inside the sheds on the water front, where the boats were hanging about waiting for fares. I expect you know the pier at Colombo. You go in under a big shed and down some steps on to the piers which are mostly under cover, with arc lamps at night. It always breaks a crowd up a bit to have to go up or down steps, and there are some gates too, where the customs birds make nuisances of themselves in an ordinary way, but this night the gates were wide open and there was no one in particular about. I don't blame them either. Hobson was with me, while Jack and Father Glennie were giving Casey and his pals a hand to move the crowd along. We reckoned, Hobson and I, that the diggers would get down the steps in batches and be easier to handle than if we had them coming down on us all at once. Also the row-boats were all waiting alongside, and we could help the diggers in pretty quickly if they weren't too fighting drunk. Luckily I had my old field notebook, so I wrote a line to Jerry to tell him what to expect, and gave it to a boatman with ten rupees, to take to the ship.

I must say I didn't feel too good. Here were about fifty men, mostly drunk, and here were Hobson and I without even a revolver. And the water was far too near to be pleasant. I knew our boys would think nothing of tossing an officer or two into the harbour, and though they would be sorry next day when sober, that wouldn't give first aid to me and Hobson. I didn't know how much they'd been drinking, but that stuff they give them in the bazaars is rank poison. Quite a little sends a man half silly, besides the effect on his inside of which as a medical man I knew all I wanted to.

Two thoughts occurred to me while we were waiting, one being what a damned fool I was to be there at all. Being a doctor it wasn't my job to look after insubordinate troops and probably get knocked on the head and drowned. But I don't see how I could have left Jack and Hobson to face the music alone. Besides the padre was there, so I'd have been lonely out of it. The other thought I had, and one which has occurred to me very forcibly and more than once, was what fools Horseferry Road were to send out a dry ship. Anyone with any experience knows that if you can get the drink you can do without it. If you can't get it, you get a craving. I'm not much of a drinker myself, except in a friendly way, but after being shut up in that boat I could have drunk anything. The diggers were worse off than we were, for they were in the lower decks, and their accommodation was about as good as what cattle might get, and you can't blame the boys if they went a bit wild when they got on shore. If they had had a rum ration every day, there wouldn't have been half this trouble. And naturally it got them a bit narked when they saw some of the officers – mostly those who were pals of Stone and Anstruther – getting a bit merry.

The crowd was gradually working down in our direction.

'Gently does it,' I said to Hobson. 'Get four or five at a time into the boats if you can, and tell the boatmen not to worry about the fares. The Colonel will have to settle them tomorrow morning, and lucky if he doesn't have a few inquests as well.'

Hobson was pretty good at a sort of pidgin-Indian, but I haven't a word, so I grabbed a kind of clerk who was standing about and told him what to say.

'Tell those black bastards,' I said, 'to take the diggers back to the boat, and if they come tomorrow the Colonel will see they get paid.'

He jabbered away to them, and then he bolted into an office and locked the door. I was just as pleased, because the boys might have been rude to him, and I knew that I would have enough to do looking after things without trying to teach them drawing-room manners.

He was only just in time, for the diggers were coming down the steps. At first it wasn't so bad. Hobson kept things going, shouting out: 'Manly boat just starting', 'All aboard for the North Shore', 'Anyone more for Mosman', and so on. The fellows from Sydney quite entered into the joke, and if they would get eight or nine into a boat that held four, well I reckoned that a nice swim in the harbour wouldn't do them any harm. I didn't think there were any sharks, but if there were, it was their trouble.

Hobson saw the boys from the other states weren't catching on too well, so he just strung together all the names he could think of, calling out in his best sergeant's parade voice: 'All aboard for Bellerive, Brown's River, Geelong, Kangaroo Island, Rottnest Island and the Great Barrier Reef.' This way all the boys from the different states felt they were getting a fair deal.

I was beginning to feel much more hopeful about things, when a bunch of men came down the steps, roaring drunk and waving bottles. I do hate a bottle. I have heard it called Australia's national weapon, which is not all just, but it is a weapon that seems to come very handy and natural to many an Australian. I was in Melbourne when they had the police strike some six or seven years ago, and I can tell you the crowd of larrikins up Elizabeth Street were laying people out with bottles as neatly as you please. That was a nasty moment, for it was after dark and they started looting shops, and there was talk of an attack on the G.P.O. But the old A.I.F. men rallied wonderfully. They flashed a message on every cinema screen in Melbourne, by which means dozens of ex-officers came rolling up as special constables and had the time of their lives. Some of our chaps had been spoiling for a scrap, and several of them that I helped to treat for scalp wounds and bruises said it was as good as having the War on again.

But, as I said, I have no special fondness for bottles.

Not only do they knock you out well and truly, but the broken glass is apt to spoil your face. I've seen men after a Saturday night in Woolloomooloo with an eye hanging right out, or their face laid right open to the gums, and I didn't fancy going back to Celia in that state.

A bunch of them saw me and Hobson and made for us, saying such things as 'Stoush the —— officers!' One great powerful fellow, a football barracker evidently from his lungs and language, kept yelling 'Ruin 'em, ruin 'em!' I've heard them shouting that at a football final till I felt pretty sick, and thanked heaven I wasn't one of the thirty-six men on the field, for a kick below the belt is over the odds.

One man had a knife and went for me, but I kicked his shin and twisted his arm and chucked the knife into a boat before he knew what had happened. Half a dozen of his pals fell in on top of him with Hobson's assistance, and were rowed away, singing somewhat rowdily. The big fellow gave poor Hobson a great whack over the head with his bottle. Luckily Hobson, being a Light Horseman, had his looped-up hat with the kangaroo feathers, so he didn't get cut, but he was knocked out for the moment. I thought the big fellow would roll him into the water, but luckily he turned on me, using some very unladylike language. Three or four of the men began jostling me, and I couldn't get my hands free, while the big fellow lifted his bottle in the air. In a second I'd have been where poor old Hobson was, peacefully asleep on the planks, when old Cavanagh butted in with a bottle in one hand and a knife in the other.

'You —— well leave the Doc alone,' he shouted. 'He's my —— cobber, the good old bastard, and the first of you buggers lays a hand on him, I'll twist his tripes for him.'

And with that he brought his bottle down with a

whack, and so did the big fellow. The bottles hit each
other in the air and smashed, and the broken glass flew
everywhere and both of them were a bit cut about the
hands and face. Well, when the boys saw this I was
afraid they'd all take sides and we'd have a free fight
among them. But their sense of humour made them see
the humorous side of things, and they laughed like a lot
of kookaburras. I'd have laughed too, but I hadn't time.
Poor old Hobson had staggered up by this time and was
walking round in circles. One of the boys gave him a
drink and they all took arms and sang 'Auld Lang Syne'.

'Well, now, boys,' I said, when they'd finished, 'you'd
better go home quietly. You'll get your medicine in the
morning all right, but I'll do what I can for you, all but
the great ugly cornstalk that laid Lieutenant Hobson out.
What were you in quod for?' I asked him quickly, not
giving him time to think.

'Did a —— bloke in, and serve him —— well right,'
said he, spitting.

'You are a —— Sunday school pet, you are,' said
Cavanagh. 'He never done a bloke in, Doc. He's just a
sneak-thief; pinched his cobbers' kit while they were up
the line and he was in billets, the dirty cow.'

The digger is much against a dirty action such as theft
of a pal's things when he isn't there. If he had really
stoushed his man, no one would have had a thing
against him, but the diggers didn't like the way he tried
to show off, making out he was better than he was, so
they just lifted him into the water. He swam about a
bit, using quite strong language, till a couple of niggers
picked him up and rowed him away.

Then one of the men shouted out: 'All aboard for
Yarra Bend,' and they all got into the boats and went off
quite happy. Yarra Bend is the big asylum at Melbourne.
I was never there, as mental cases aren't in my line, but

127

I have been over it, and it is first-rate of its kind. I never much fancied being a doctor in a loony-bin myself, but it is meat and drink to some. The diggers were still a bit sozzled, but they have wonderfully strong heads, and their voices sounded very pretty on the water as they sang 'Swanee River' and 'The Old Folks at Home', with a few interruptions.

Hobson and I went up the steps, through the empty sheds. At the top we met Jack Howe and Casey rounding up the stragglers. Jack had a cattle station away up somewhere in Queensland, and men and bullocks are much the same once you get them on the move. Keep them going and don't let them straggle and you are all right. Father Glennie was tying up some broken heads, and roaring them up at the same time. I judged I could safely leave his lambs to his care, so Hobson and I went into the G.O.H. and had a drink, and then Jack came back and we had one on him and one on me, and of course Hobson couldn't be left out, so we had one on him. Then Father Glennie came in, and we wanted him to have one on the house, but he would only have tea.

'You can't have a Johnny Woodser, Father,' I said. 'We'll all have tea, and it will be on me.'

So we all sat there and had some tea, and we agreed the digger isn't a bad chap if decently handled. There were little outbreaks in the street from time to time, but they were not more than our military police could deal with. Some of the M.P.'s were a bit rough with the boys that night, which all led to bad blood later. By about midnight the street was quite peaceful and we all turned in. I found Celia still awake. The poor kid had been worrying a bit, but she is wonderfully brave and sensible and she knows I can look after myself all right. Also the mosquitoes had been keeping her awake. So I hunted round and found a hole in the net, so I pinned it up with a hairpin and killed two big brutes that had got inside. Then I turned the punkah off, because in hotels they will put it right over the bed where you are apt to get chills and earaches and stiff necks, and we soon enjoyed a good night's rest.

8

Jerry hands it to the Colonel

Everyone was a bit late next morning, except the Browns
and their kiddies who had gone off to early service somewhere. I am quite a religious man myself in my quiet
way, having thought very deeply on some subjects, but
early service is a thing I have no use for. My old dad was
the same, and I've heard him say all men were welcome
to think as they damn well pleased so long as no parson
came snooping round 'his' place. He was a wonderfully
broadminded man, the old dad.

We were all wondering at breakfast whether the ship
would be delayed because of last night's little bust-up,
but Jack Howe, who had been out getting a line on
things, said the authorities were only too glad to get rid
of us at any price, and were hurrying up the loading of
the ship. All claims against the 'Rudolstadt' were to
be settled by the Australian Government, he said, but
whether they were I don't know, as I seemed to lose
interest in the matter. I don't worry much about govern-
ments, though of course I'd do my damnedest to put
Labor out any day. I once went over the Parliament
Library in Sydney and had some quite interesting side-
lights on affairs, seeing the kind of books various members
took out. As for Billy Hughes, well his day is over, but he
deserves mention in that he made such good subjects for
Dyson and Low. I once saw Billy Hughes dance the
Lancers at Government House, Melbourne, the time the

Prince of Wales was out, and I've never enjoyed a dance so much. But I don't meddle with politics – they're a dirty game.

Hobson was none the worse for his knock on the head, those Light Horsemen being hard cases. We were to be on board by midday, and presently some of the officers blew in from the Galle Face. They had been told we were all killed and had come round to see the corpses, so they stood us drinks. All agreed that unless the Colonel took serious steps we would have a pretty rough passage, but all also agreed that he was not likely to do so, thus getting nowhere. They said they had had a bonzer dance the night before, there being several Australians at the Galle Face who were coming on our boat.

Mrs Dicky shortly turned up with a couple of young officers. She and I and Celia got yarning in a corner of the lounge, and Mrs Dicky told us all about the dance. She had found some old friends and had a fine time. She said Mrs Henley and Captain Smith had been dancing all evening again and she wouldn't be surprised if he left the boat and stayed on at Colombo. Everyone had been interested about them, but no one knew much, as they had been very reserved. I am a reserved sort of chap myself, but one should take part in what is going on, as if all were to keep shut up like clams it would be a dull sort of life.

When Celia and Mrs Dicky went upstairs to look at Celia's shopping, I was left alone for a bit, and who should happen to come in and sit quite near me but the very identical couple. I was half behind a table with a big palm on it and sitting well down in one of those big cane chairs, and anyway they wouldn't have noticed if I had been General Monash himself. I could see with half an eye that dope was his trouble, there was no doubt at all. It is a funny thing, our fellows are very few of them given that way. They may drink a lot, but doping is a habit very few of them seem to get. And even the amount they drink is greatly exaggerated. Look, I have known hundreds of fellows one way or another since 1914, thousands you might really say, but very few of them were real drinkers. A whole lot of the A.I.F. men liked tea better than anything, but there are many times in a war when beer is easier to get and quicker to drink than tea. It used to drive the diggers wild the way the families in the French billets drank coffee. They didn't seem to have the ghost of a notion how to make a decent cup of tea.

I could hear what Smith and Mrs Henley were saying, and I suppose I ought to have got up, or coughed or something, but I didn't do it at the start, and then I didn't seem to find an opportunity. It is often the way that if you do not do a thing at once it seems to be more difficult to do it afterwards. There was a chap I met at Bullecourt who lives up the North Shore Line at Turramurra, and I've been meaning to look him up ever since 1920, but I haven't managed it yet and I daresay I never will. He was a dull sort of a chap, mostly interested in wool-buying. But it shows how if you put a thing off it doesn't seem to happen.

As far as I could hear he was asking her if he could come on as far as Singapore with her, and she was turning him down. He said he would do any blessed thing in the world for her, and she said if he couldn't give it up there was nothing doing. I concluded that 'it' meant the dope, and as things turned out I was right.

'If you will leave Henry and come with me, I'll never touch it again,' he said, with his face all twitching.

'Henry is a perfectly good husband except that I don't care for him,' she said, 'and I am not going to leave Henry for a drug-fiend, even if I do love him like hell.'

I felt more than ever that I ought to be somewhere else, but it was getting more difficult to move every minute.

'You say you love me and you won't raise a finger to help me,' said Smith in a husky kind of voice.

'I know exactly what you are,' said Mrs Henley, and you'd have thought she was talking about the weather. 'You are going straight to the devil, and if I were alone I'd come too. But I'm not going to let Henry down. I shall forget you some day. You will forget me even sooner, and that is quite a good revenge for you. It hurts me even now to think how easily you will forget.'

He started in to try to explain, but she got up and said she would come down to the pier and see him off. I slipped away then to fetch Celia, but I felt uncomfortable about what I had heard. We didn't need a dope fiend to make the rest of the voyage more pleasant, especially one that had just been turned down by a woman and would naturally be a bit peeved. However, there's no sense in looking for troubles, so I collected Celia and Mrs Dicky and the shopping, and we went down to the pier. It is only a step from the G.O.H. to the waterfront, and as Mrs Henley and Smith were just in front, it was difficult not to get near them. However, I did say to Mrs Dicky I thought there was trouble ahead of us, and being a brainy little woman she got on to what I meant at once. Smith was yarning away to Mrs Henley, and I guessed he was trying to worry her again. I didn't know if it was my business quite, but I chipped in and said:

'Can you go over with my missis and Mrs Dicky, Skipper? I've got one or two jobs I must do.'

He looked at me as if he would eat me, but Mrs Henley said:

'Of course he will. Good-bye, Captain Smith.'

She shook hands, and he looked at her the way I've seen a man look when he has had a bad stomach wound and you are going to give him a shot of morphia.

'Good-bye, think of me in hell,' he said. 'I'll go there now as fast as I can.'

The other ladies were getting into the boat, so they didn't hear this, and they didn't hear her say 'You will forget', which she said in quite a laughing kind of way. The boat went off and I waited a minute to see if I was wanted, but she said:

'Thanks, Major Bowen, I am not going to faint. Good-bye.'

And off she walked. I saw a woman once, up in the Mallee, her two kids had gone off into the bush and got lost. They got a black tracker at last and found them after three days, but of course the poor kiddies were dead. Mrs Henley had the same look that woman had. I never heard of her again, and don't know what happened to her. No one could help Smith except himself, and she did the decent thing in sticking to her husband. The little job I had mentioned was really an invention, so I got a boat and went off to the ship. I had a feeling there would be plenty to do on board, and such proved to be the case.

The first thing I did, I saw that Celia and Mrs Dicky were all right. Mrs Dicky said Smith had been a bit glum at first, but he had brightened up wonderfully and made himself agreeable to them both.

'I suppose you won't mind if he flirts with Celia,' said Mrs Dicky.

'His troubles,' I said, knowing Celia would turn him down well and truly if he became a nuisance. 'What about you, Mrs Dicky?'

But she only laughed.

The man I wanted was Jerry, and after hunting in the

smoke-room and lounge and on the boat deck, I found him forward, leaning over the railing, looking down into the well deck.

'Well, old son,' I said, 'how goes it?'

'Like a singed possum,' said Jerry. 'That was a pretty lot you sent us on board last night. Old Doc Bird has been picking bits of glass out of them ever since, and half the men are like the morning after the night before.'

'I don't blame them,' I said. 'If it hadn't been for Father Glennie and Jack Howe and a few others, there'd have been no morning after for some of us, and particularly for Hobson.'

Then Jerry started in to tell me all about the night before. He and Stanley, the one that had the French wife that was going to have a kid, had been on duty that evening. The men were all pretty noisy, because their cobbers kept on bringing beer from shore, and though no one was actually tight, they were all pretty merry. The Colonel had had a locksmith to make new keys for the cells and there was a guard to see the men didn't interfere. Well, they didn't interfere, but when the keys were finished they just took them and chucked them into the harbour. The Colonel was wild and said he would have a court-martial the following day, but the officers didn't pay much attention, as they had him pretty well sized up, poor old fellow. Picky wasn't a bad sort really, but he had no more guts than a Portugoose, and as for Anderson he jumped like a frog if anyone spoke to him. All that day he had kept out of the way of the diggers as much as he could, and whenever he poked his nose on deck, some of the boys would start singing 'If you were the only girl in the world', and Andy would pretend he didn't hear. Jerry said it beat the band.

Well, it seems as evening came on the men began dropping in by twos and threes, some the worse for drink, some just happy. Most of them had bought a lot of stuff in the bazaars, souvenirs and so on, and silks for their girls, and some of them got dropped into the water and there was some little ill-feeling, the boatmen being largely blamed for what occurred. But, as Jerry said, an Indian boatman hasn't the physique of our fellows and cannot be expected to get a digger and all his parcels up the ship's ladder on his own. Our boys said the boatmen had made them drop the parcels so that they could pick them out of the water and take them home, but from what I have seen of troops coming on board after a spree, I should say they were quite able to drop their parcels without asking anyone's help.

Anyway, things calmed down a bit and the boys got singing down on the well deck, and Jerry and Stanley began to congratulate themselves that their troubles were over, when a boat came alongside and a nigger in it with a yarn about wanting to see the Colonel. The corporal on duty took him along to old Picking, and no one knows what Picking made of it all, but luckily the corporal, who was an old soldier, knew a bit of the language and understood the man to say he had a letter. So the letter being addressed to Jerry, they sent for him.

'And I can tell you I fairly got the wind up,' said Jerry. 'Old Picking kept on saying "What shall we do", and Andy was as little good as a sick cow, so I told the old Colonel he'd better leave it to me, and I told Andy if he showed his pretty face on the troop decks that night I'd eat up what was left of him.'

Then Jerry and Stanley raided some of the cabins to look for revolvers, but could only raise three or four, which they gave to a few fellows they could rely on. Jerry then went in to tell Mrs Jerry not to be frightened, but he had better have left things alone, for young Dick had just gone off to sleep and when Jerry came in and turned

136

the light on he woke him up. Mrs Jerry fairly hit the roof. From what Jerry told me, I don't think he had ever been so strafed. She said the ship could be full of drunken murderers if it liked, but the first one that came into the cabin she would tell him off well and truly, and if Jerry wanted to be a murderer too, that was the way to do it, coming banging into the cabin just when the child was going to sleep. Mary was in the other cabin and the nurse was ashore for the night with some friends, so Mrs Jerry had the place to herself, and she fairly ran the old Colonel out of the cabin and told him next time he came in he could take his boots off.

'Since when', Jerry said, 'I've not had my boots off all night.'

So having done all he could to make Mrs Jerry happy and comfortable, Jerry went down to D deck where the rude and licentious soldiery were beginning to come aboard. These were the men who had been in the rickshaw riots and down on the steps. Most of these had bottles, but luckily full ones, and Jerry reckoned they would have the sense not to stoush anyone with a bottle while there was any beer in it. There were one or two making themselves objectionable, but Stanley and a couple of good sergeants hustled them off to the cells. A sergeant was put on sentry, and though there were no keys, the men weren't too drunk to recognize a guard with a gun when they saw one.

The next thing that came along was the boat-load that had the big fellow in it that had tried to do me in. When they came up to the ship Jerry saw he would have to stand by for trouble. He said it took four men to get that big fellow – Heenan his name was, a Mick of course – and one sergeant had lost a tooth and another had a black eye before they had finished. Things were then fairly peaceful till daylight, but Jerry stayed up all night, being one who took no chances. The crew grumbled a bit at the mess, but some of the boys gave them a hand in clearing away the blood and glass and things, and by the time I got on board the ship looked fairly clean – which was all she ever was.

We left Colombo shortly after midday, and I should say the name of Australia was none too popular there for some time to come. After lunch Colonel Picking had an officers' meeting and put Andy up to asking for a court-martial for the men who were in the shavoo the night before, but Jerry shut him up well and truly.

'See here, Mr Anderson,' said he in a very cutting and sarcastic way, 'if this were a girls' school we'd ask you to be the teacher, but it isn't, and what's more it's high time you got some horse sense. Our job is to get these troops back to Australia with as few casualties as possible. How can you have a court-martial with hundreds of men in a mutinous state and not enough of us to keep them in order? They'll laugh at you, and very likely cut your throat later.'

No one could deny this, so no one said anything.

'And another thing,' said Jerry, 'what weapons have we got? Will you give orders, sir,' he said to Colonel Picking, 'for all offcers to bring their revolvers in here, now, and take stock?'

The Colonel looked surprised, but he was only too glad to anything Jerry said, so he ordered all present to get their guns and bring them to his cabin right-away. I never had one, having had mine borrowed, as I believe I mentioned before, in France, so I just waited. I could see Jerry had something up his sleeve, but whether it was a white rabbit, or what, I couldn't say.

Well, I soon knew, as one man after another came back empty handed. Higgins was on sentry-go at the door, so it didn't matter his hearing, but the language was all of a quite violent kind. The only ones who had their guns were the ones who had been on duty the night before. Of those who had been on shore, not one could find his anywhere.

'What's the joke?' said one of them to Jerry.

'You bet your sweet life it's no joke,' Jerry said. 'I'm only proving to you that you can't have a court-martial. What happened is that some of the bad eggs went through the officers' quarters last night. I had my suspicions, and now I know. It was a nice neat job, waiting till everyone was ashore and then going through the cabins. I daresay they borrowed some other little things as well. That shows what the guard is like. Christ!' he said, in a nasty voice that made little Nancy jump, 'some of you deserve to get your revolvers pinched, and if it weren't for the women and kiddies, I'd say you all do.'

Jerry then spoke his opinion on a few things. He was nice and respectful to old Picking, but it was easy to see that Picking would have been elsewhere were it possible. So Jerry put it to Picking, what were we to do. There were about six revolvers among us, besides what a few of the sergeants might have, and the whole ship, as you might say, against us, with God knows how many guns. When Jerry had finished his piece, Colonel Picking asked him what we were to do. So Jerry said the guard must consist in future entirely of sergeants, and the officers must take over all sentry duty, etc. There was a lot of arguing one way and another, but it was settled the way Jerry wanted it at the end. I left them at it, as I had to go to the surgery.

When I got down, I found old Doc Bird in among the kiddies' food.

'Did I tell you I'd get more of this patent stuff on at Colombo, Tom?' he said.

'That's right,' I said.

He let out a kind of a groan. To make a long story short, he had got a bit muddled and given his orderly who went on shore the wrong instructions. The patent food was there all right, but he had only ordered about two-thirds of what I had told him we needed.

'Well, Doc,' I said, 'we'll have to do what we can with condensed milk from the ship's stores and fruit juice. Thank the Lord it's only as far as Fremantle.'

I could have kicked myself for not standing over him while he wrote out the order, but there was my chit, quite O.K., and if the old chump had to go copying it out wrong, who could ever have expected a thing like that?

'Fruit juice?' he said. 'There's no fruit come aboard as far as I know.'

Here I became quite annoyed and sent a fellow to find Higgins.

'See here, Higgins,' I said when he came along, 'what about that fruit we were to take on board?'

'Excuse me, sir,' Higgins said, 'but the troops got it all.'

'Holy Cripes,' I said, and settled myself comfortably to hear the rest.

'It was this way, sir,' Higgins said. 'The troops were a bit above themselves what with the little turn-up last night and all the drink they'd had, so when the boats with the fruit came alongside this morning, they got down to the ladder, and they just borrowed everything as it came aboard.'

'And where the devil is it now?' I asked.

'Well, sir,' Higgins said, 'some they ate, the diggers being very fond of fruit. All the squashy ones they threw at the Indians, sir, and the rest is in their cabins.'

I was so angry I made for the door. It was a silly thing to do, and Higgins stopped me.

'Excuse me, sir,' he said, 'but I wouldn't go to the men's quarters, not at present. Have you your revolver, sir?'

'Oh,' I said, sitting down again, 'you know about that too, do you?'

Higgins opened the door and looked out. Then he stuck his head suddenly out of the window on to the deck, but no one was there, so he told us what Jerry had guessed already, namely that some of the diggers had been through our quarters last night. He said they were real professionals that did the job, and they'd got the guns without disturbing the cabins, all quite neat and quiet.

'All but the one who went to Colonel Fairchild's cabin, sir,' said Higgins with a grin. 'He didn't know Mrs Fairchild was there, and he came out quicker than he went in.'

I must say I was tickled by the idea of some great husky fellow getting ticked off by Mrs Jerry, and had to laugh very heartily.

'Well, Doc,' I said, 'how are we going to feed those poor kiddies, I don't yet see, but something we've got to do.'

'I managed to save a case of oranges for you, sir,' said Higgins. 'It's in the first-class surgery where the troops aren't likely to go, and I labelled it Castor Oil.'

He was a great little fellow, Higgins.

Well, I may say that I hope never to have to feed a lot of kidddies on insufficient rations again, but we managed. Higgins scrounged round for condensed milk, and I did quite a lot of research work on cornflour and biscuits and things, boiled with a little sugar, and we had the oranges, and we kept the poor little beggars going, but some of them got a horrid pasty look and made me feel like a murderer. I may as well say that whatever else may have happened at Fremantle, I saw to it that we got proper supplies of food on for the kiddies. Old Doc Bird wasn't too pleased at my butting in, but though he was a dear old fellow, I didn't think he was the man to be trusted on the job.

Further trouble for the medical staff shortly eventuated. I mentioned that we took on some new passengers at Colombo. There was a Captain Peel and his wife and two kiddies. He was a very sick man, having had some sort of fever in India, and about the colour of made mustard. I will say for old Doc Bird that he knew a lot about fever, and by the time we got to Sydney Peel was a different man. His wife had been a hospital nurse, a type I never much appreciate in private life, as they either have no children and think it will interest you to know exactly why, or else if they have kiddies they tell you about your confinements, which is no treat to a doctor. I thought these kiddies – a nice little boy and girl they were – looked a bit off colour, but put it down to India and thought no more. However, two days later they had temperatures and spots. Doc Bird said measles, and I daresay he was right. One infantile spot looked much like another to me in those days. Now it's different, though even so I am bound to say that there are times when you can't tell German measles from the other sorts. But the mothers always know, so I let them choose till I can say definitely which it is.

So there we were with two infectious cases and no warning given. I must say it was the one lucky thing that did happen on that voyage that no one else got it. Providence must have been thinking of something else at the time, or we could surely have had a nice run of measles through the ship.

Celia and Mrs Dicky had had measles more than once, so they gave a hand with the nursing. We rigged up some kind of quarantine with sheets and disinfectants and did what we could and didn't make a fuss, and lots of the passengers never knew what was happening. The kiddies had it very lightly, but even so the heat was considerable, and I felt very sorry for the poor little beggars shut up in that cabin all day. Celia and Mrs Dicky helped to keep them amused, and it all helped to pass the time away. Mrs Peel wasn't much help. She had had her kiddies too late in life and was like a fussy old hen with them.

I haven't said much about Stone and Anstruther lately. As a matter of fact they had been mostly in their men's quarters, doing instruction and physical jerks, and were getting a bit fed up with the whole affair. Stone had gone on the jag at Colombo and was lying low for a few days. He had bought about sixty of those big coloured straw hats and given them to all his friends. Young Dick had lost his topee overboard and then he lost four hats that Stone gave him, and it wasn't till Jerry had found him trying to push a deck chair over the railing that he realized the way the hats had gone. After that young Dick had to think up other ways of getting into mischief.

I'll never forget the night Stone was so dead to the world that it was all Hobson and I could do to hold him upright against the boat deck railing while the Old Man stood and yarned to us about the stars. Celia came out strong with some first-class ideas about stars which she said she had learned at school, surprising the Old Man considerably. Stone was very grateful afterwards, as he said he would have felt quite mortified to be discovered in such a condition by the Merchant Service. He was a good old sort and we used to meet him at balls at Government House subsequently, but he left the navy and took up land, and I haven't heard of him for donkey's years.

The atmosphere was pretty thick on board those days,

143

as you may well imagine. What with the diggers half
mutinous and at daggers drawn with the crew, measles in
the first class, a colonel that couldn't command and an
adjutant that everyone laughed at, no refrigerator, not
enough kiddies' food, and not knowing where our revolvers were, we had our troubles. I may add that the water
was being rationed and half the women weren't on
speaking terms, but these were just frills as you might
say.

Smith, the Indian army chap, was making pretty good
running with some of the ladies. He was that kind of
man that seems to have a certain attraction for women,
though this is not a type that appeals to me much. Per-
sonally I do not see that a man has any call to mess about
with women. I have had many good girl pals in my time,
both at school and at the University, and later, but we
were just pals, and none of this love-making business
with married women. I must admit, though, it is not
always the man's fault. Some women, in spite of having
a good husband and a home, seem to wish to carry on
with flirtations even after they are married. Of course I
like a woman to be friendly, and it is nice to know some
cultivated and humorous women who can take a joke
and yet talk seriously about such subjects as the wool
sales, or the Sydney Harbour bridge. But I have a great
feeling of respect for married women and find the
English men somewhat wanting in a feeling of reverence.

But Smith was in trouble, poor chap, and one cannot
blame him. Anyone who is taking as much dope as he
was is hardly normal. For two or three days he was
always with the French girl, the one I mentioned in the
three-berth cabin. Then they had some sort of a row and
he began to run after Mrs Dicky. She was a clever little
woman with her wits about her, and she gave the office
to Celia, and those two were together morning, noon

144

and night, so that Smith could never get Mrs Dicky to himself. You would think I might have found it a bit of a nuisance always to have Mrs Dicky around with Celia, but what with the two surgeries and one thing and another I hardly had a free moment all day and was only too glad for Celia to have a pal and amuse herself. Jack Howe's wife was with them too a good bit, but Smith hadn't much time for her. He had never seen her play poker, or he would have had more interest in her.

9

The Rabbit's Funeral

We were now due to arrive at Fremantle in two days. It was hot and damp and things were unpleasant all round. I am no drinker myself, but to drink nothing but ginger beer and lemonade does a man no good, besides being bloating. The diggers had got through the beer they brought on at Colombo and were in a sullen and disobliging state.

It was a hot sunny day when I came up on deck before breakfast, and the first thing I noticed was the sun was in the wrong place. I am pretty observant in many ways and there is very little that goes on that escapes me, though I am not one to make a song about it. And when you have been used to see the sun rising on one side of the ship, it comes as somewhat of a shock to find it rising on the other. I find it somewhat difficult to describe my exact sensations at this sight. When first I stepped out on deck it struck me that the outlook was a little different to ordinary. Somehow things did not look quite similar. I have often noticed that the light makes a great difference to things. Take for instance Sydney Harbour. It looks at early morning quite other to what it does at sunset, this being owing to the sunlight coming from the east rather than from the west. In like manner a patch of bush by evening light will almost appear a different place than it is at midday.

I puzzled over this for a bit, in the way one does when

he is not giving his mind to a thing, but it was not for several seconds that the idea dawned on me that it was not the sun that was acting differently to usual, but the boat. The only feasible explanation was that the boat had turned round in the night, though this I could hardly believe. Just then Stone came along. He being a sailor, I asked him what was happening.

'See here, old son,' I said, 'am I mad, or is the ship mad, or has the world gone upside down?'

'You and the world are all right,' he said. 'It's the ship that is wrong. Haven't you heard?'

'Heard what?' I said.

'Damaged steering gear, or propeller, I don't yet know which,' he said. 'Wait a bit and you'll see she's going round in circles.' Sure enough, the poor 'Rudolstadt' was making a big sweep right round, and by the time the breakfast bugle went, the sun was shining on the right side again. I went down to breakfast, but no one seemed to have any idea of what had happened. They were all eating away as cheerfully as if we had been full steam ahead. Anyway it didn't seem to be my job to call attention to the fact that we would probably be delayed in getting to Fremantle, so I said nothing. Celia and Mrs Dicky were just finishing their breakfast, so I told them to look out when they got on deck and see if they saw anything funny.

When I got on deck again I found them both sitting aft with Mrs Jerry and the kids. Celia started in to roar me up for pulling their legs, when young Dick who was perched up on the rail, sang out:

'Why is the boat going all crooked, Uncle Tom?'

'How do you mean, crooked?' said Mrs Jerry. 'I hope to goodness we aren't going all on one side again.'

For I quite forgot to mention that halfway between

Aden and Colombo the stokers had had words over something and didn't trim the coal properly. Consequently we
were two days with a good list to port, which amused the
kids, but no one else saw the joke, especially the stewards
who had to carry plates and dishes all on the slant. The
trouble was soon got over, but it was not one which we
wished to recur.

'Look, Uncle Tom,' said young Dick, pointing behind
the boat.

We all got up to have a look, and I haven't seen a
sight like that since we were dodging submarines in the
early days of the War. I have a wonderful feeling for the
poetical side of life at times, and much appreciate nature,
and somehow the long line of a ship's wake seems to me
somewhat like the furrow made by a big tractor plough
in the wheat country. But anyone who had driven a
tractor like the wake we saw would have lost his job
quick and lively. It was more like a snake, one of those
big ones you see away in the bush, or a corkscrew. For
the second time that day I began to wonder if I was
seeing straight, but there was no getting away from the
fact. The 'Rudolstadt' wasn't going round in circles now,
but she was a sick boat, and was altering her course
every few moments till, as already stated, it reminded
me of nothing so much as dodging submarines in the
Mediterranean.

Leaving Celia and the kids, I made my way to the
smoke-room, thinking I might find Jerry there, as indeed
I did. He had been down in the engine-room having a
yarn with Schultz. He said what old Schultz had said
about the Germans and the hot-water pipes was nothing
to what he was saying about the Germans and the propeller. He was putting the fear of God into all his staff
and working full speed to try to patch things up, so Jerry
told us, but he wouldn't know for some hours if he could

fix things up the way we would get to Fremantle on time, or even under our own power.

I need hardly say that when I got down to the surgery I learnt through Higgins that the news was all over the men's quarters and they were laying money on when we'd get to Fremantle. A lot of them were pretty fed up about the whole affair, and it hadn't improved their tempers. I saw the Old Man once, looking like the Hymn of Hate, but it didn't seem to me a good moment for having a yarn with him.

I was kept pretty busy in the surgery that morning with small casualties, as some of the engine-room hands working on the propeller shaft had got a bit knocked about. There was an unpleasant incident when I was treating one of the crew for a smashed finger, when Cavanagh came in with a couple of sergeants. It was a bit of a joke with those guards. They knew they couldn't do much with the prisoners, and the prisoners knew it too, so they all got on pretty well. But if Cavanagh came up to the surgery for treatment he liked to do things properly, so he always got a couple of the guard to bring him, arguing that as they had got him crimed they ought to do their bit in giving him an escort. He had been having an argument with young Casey, and not realizing that Casey was a lightweight boxer, he had got his face knocked about and I was attending to it for him. I was busy at the store cupboard, getting out some fresh strapping, and I missed the beginning of the discussion, but it seems that Cavanagh had passed some remark about the engineers being a lazy lot of swine.

This was not pleasing to the engineer, who told Cavanagh it was no pleasure to him and his mates to sweat their guts out in a blanky Hun boat to get a lot of illegitimate Australians back to their blanky homes. You will understand that these were not the exact words he used, which were indeed quite offensive. But Cavanagh was quite annoyed and some very fierce language was exchanged. I told the guards they'd better take Cavanagh away.

'All right, Doc, I'm going home,' Cavanagh said, 'but don't you be surprised if you hear some news from the crew's quarters before long.'

I only laughed at him, for he looked like nothing on earth with his face covered with strapping, but it was nothing to laugh about really, as you will hear.

It was about midday when I got on deck again. There was a little crowd over where we usually sat, so I went up to have a look. Celia saw me and came to meet me.

'I'm glad you've come, Tom,' she said. 'Captain Smith has been very queer all morning and I think he has been drinking. Mrs Dicky can manage him as a rule, but she can't do anything with him today. Mrs Howe is there too, but he is behaving in such an extraordinary way that we don't know what to do. And if we try to go away he begs us to stay, and says he will jump into the sea.'

When I heard that I knew there was no danger. Once a fellow starts in to talk about suicide, you may bet your life he won't do anything about it. The ones that do kill themselves are the ones that keep quiet and cheerful, and one morning you wake up to find them with their throats cut, or all curled up through drinking disinfectant.

'What sort of a way is he behaving?' I asked.

Celia became a rather pretty pink colour.

'He said he would show us some curios,' she said, 'and when he began to tell us how he got them, he got rather funny. All about India and China it was and we aren't sure if we ought to understand or not, so we are glad you came.'

That did get my goat. If a man has no more natural respect for women than to talk in a way which may cause them discomfort, he deserves a good hiding. I like a good broad story myself, especially if there is genuine humour in it, which is a thing that always appeals to me, but I wouldn't tell one to Celia, or anyway not the sort she oughtn't to understand. Though my little missis is no wowser and can take a joke very well.

All the same it was going to be a bit awkward, for you can't exactly knock a man down on hearsay, and after all Smith might have been only pulling their legs. However I thought I'd better go and see.

Now, to explain exactly what happened, Smith was standing with his back to the rail. Mrs Dicky and Mrs Howe were facing him as he was showing them some kind of curio, Celia joined them again, and I think Mrs Jerry was there, and the nice French girl, Mrs Stanley. As I have before mentioned I am a good height, and could easily see over the heads of the women on to Smith's hand. As I came up he said to Mrs Dicky:

'Here's some Chinese carving, something you'll like, Mrs Dicky,' and held out his hand for her to see.

Well, I've done physiology and I've done Cairo pretty thoroughly, and I've read a bit about Indian carvings and temple pictures, but anything like that little carving I've never seen. Mrs Dicky and Mrs Howe were nearest him, so that Celia and Mrs Jerry couldn't see for the moment. Mrs Dicky was a good little sport and up to most things, but she went quite white and gasped. I was going to interfere when Mrs Howe put out her hand and said as cool as you please:

'Oh, do let me see it, Captain Smith.'

He gave it to her, smiling in a stupid sort of way. I suppose he thought she'd get a nasty shock, and he was in that state of mind when to frighten anyone would give him sincere pleasure. Those dope fiends sometimes get like that. It is also called Sadism, after a French vicomte

or something of the sort called de Sade. His life, which
I have read with great interest from a medical point of
view, is certainly not suitable for all, but it throws much
light on many things.

Mrs Howe took the carving in her hand. You'd have
sworn it was some artistic carving of a flower or a bird,
the way she looked at it as if she were pleased and
interested. Then she dropped it into the sea.

'Oh, dear, I've dropped it,' she said. 'I hope it doesn't
matter.'

I've seen some pretty good poker players in my time.
Once when I was fossicking round near the osmiridium
fields in Tasmania one vacation, I saw a man called
Pete Barker, though his real name I believe was Joe
Stevens or Stevenson, lose all the cash he'd got and all
the osmiridium he'd found in six months, and his swag
and his bluey. But he bluffed the whole gang in the end
on three sevens and a pair of Jacks and got the lot back.
But Mrs Howe had them all beat. She just looked as if
she had dropped a cigarette overboard accidentally and
wanted another.

Smith went a nasty purple colour, and I judged the
women had about done their whack by then and it was
time a man took over the job. So I said:

'Tough luck, Skipper. Come and have a drink on me.'

He came along in a dazed sort of way and I took him
to his cabin and gave him a hypodermic and I got
Higgins to keep an eye on him till he went off. After
that he just lay in his cabin and filled himself up with
dope, and I didn't see the sense of interfering, because
you can't break a man of doping in two days, especially
when you have no military authority over him. The two
chaps who were in his cabin were good sorts and they
took it in turns to sit with him and listen to what he
had to say. From the little I heard I should say he could

have given de Sade a pretty good handicap in some ways. I was a bit uneasy as to what he might say about Mrs Henley, but after I'd heard half an hour of his talk I realized that if his lady friends had been lined up, it would have been not unlike the opening of David Jones's sale in Sydney. I was glad of this, as I had a great respect for Mrs Henley who showed much common sense in turning him down.

That afternoon there was to be a boxing contest, down in the well deck forward, between some of the diggers and some of the naval ratings. We were expecting young Casey to do pretty well, and but for the fact that he had skinned one of his knuckles on Cavanagh's teeth, he was in tip-top form. I roared him up well and truly for wasting his good skin on an Aussie when he could have a naval rating to practise on. It would certainly have been more pleasant for all if the ship had been going straight, as it was very upsetting for the boxers not to know where the sun would be next.

The boxing was timed for 3.30 p.m. After lunch most of us were below helping with the preparations. Celia and Mrs Howe were reading on deck, almost alone. Mrs Jerry was in her cabin reading to the kids, and Mrs Dicky was getting over some hysterics that she'd had after Smith's departure. I didn't see what happened, but I got it all from Celia, and in a way I'm glad I wasn't there or there might have been murder.

Celia said she and Mrs Howe were sitting reading quietly, when they heard a bit of a row forward, where the steps outside the smoke-room go down to the troops' deck. But being by now quite used to rows they took no notice. The row, as I afterwards found when the man came round to the surgery to have a broken rib set, was the sentry being helped none to courteously down the steps by a mob of diggers. They were in a kind of pro-

153

cession, with black bands round their arms, carrying something and singing a sad song, when Celia who is very musical says was called 'The place where the old horse died'. They all came marching slowly along, singing this sad song till they got to where Celia was. She didn't know whether to be frightened, or to think it was a lark, poor kid. Mrs Howe asked what it was all about.

The procession stopped and no one seemed to know what to say. They were all nudging each other the way kids do when they know they've taken the tap out of the water tank and none of them likes to be the first to mention it. Then young Casey said:

'It's the funeral, mum.'

'What funeral?' Mrs Howe said.

'The rabbit's, mum.'

Then they all started in to explain that they hadn't been any too pleased with the rations lately, and today there was some rabbit that was the limit. Of course some Australians are particular about eating rabbits and won't look at them. This is after all only prejudice, as a rabbit is very nice in a pie with plenty of fat bacon, though I admit boiled rabbit is one of those things which no one would wish to think about again. When I was a kid the people in Melbourne and Sydney wouldn't eat rabbit unless they were really poor, but now you see them in all the good delicatessen shops. About the lowest thing you could do was to push a barrow around the suburbs of Sydney, shouting 'Rab-bee, rab-bee'. C. J. Dennis has some poetry about that, I think.

But as far as this rabbit went it does not seem to have been entirely prejudice, for Casey very kindly offered Celia and Mrs Howe to smell it. Celia said when he took the lid off the dish they were carrying, that was

154

quite enough. She and Mrs Howe just got up and went away. Also they were a bit scared of the mob.

The boys naturally thought this a good joke, and the procession went on, a bit more noisy than before, partly owing to a weedy little chap who played the accordion very well called Peters falling over Celia's deck chair, for which I had to treat a crushed finger later. Celia said she and Mrs Howe were standing in the door that led to the first-class companion way, then the procession stopped again. She heard Mrs Jerry's voice out of her cabin window asking what the matter was.

Young Casey began to explain, but Mrs Jerry went right off the handle again. Celia said she had always had a great respect for Mrs Jerry ever since she was a kid, but she had never really understood her before. She just went for those diggers bald-headed. She said she wasn't going to have her kids disturbed when they were asleep after lunch for all the bad rabbits in Australia, and the first one that opened his mouth she'd report him to Colonel Fairchild. Of course none of them wanted this, for old Jerry was quite the most popular man I've ever known among the men.

'Are any of you men married?' she said.

All the single men pushed the married ones to the front.

'All right,' said Mrs Jerry, 'you know what it is to get the kids off to sleep, and you know exactly what your wives say if you wake them up, so you know exactly what's coming to you from me, and it will be much worse than what the Colonel gets.'

The diggers were of course delighted at the idea of old Jerry getting ticked off for waking the kids, and became very good-humoured.

'You married ones can tell the single ones,' said Mrs Jerry. 'Is that Casey I see there?'

Casey was well behind by that time among the single men, but his cobbers pushed him up to the front again, where Mrs Jerry roared him up for being in a rabbit shop when he ought to be thinking of the fight. Young Casey quite got the wind up. Then Mrs Jerry told them to take that rabbit round to the other side before she started losing her temper.

Those fellows went past her window like mice, Celia said, but when they got round on the starboard side they made up for it by having a football match with the rabbit. Casey told me about that afterwards. Some of it got thrown overboard, and some got trodden into the deck, and someone put the head down the ventilator that went to Stone and Anstruther's cabin on C deck. Stone was resting on his berth when the rabbit's face came in, and Catchpole who was passing told me afterwards he'd never heard any one use such peculiar language as Mr Stone.

Of course we knew nothing of this till afterwards. The boxing began at 3.30 p.m. according to schedule, and young Casey turned up all right. There weren't any very remarkable fights, but some of our men put up quite a good show. Stone's men won on points and altogether it was a very enjoyable affair. The Old Man gave away the prizes and did his best to appear interested, but it was evident that he had something on his mind. Knowing the condition the ship was in, I was hardly surprised. It was a piece of good luck that he didn't know about the rabbit on his deck, or he might have stopped the fight.

We had naturally been looking at the ring and not out to sea, so it was not till the prizes had been given that we saw a big boat with the Orient funnels steaming past us at no very great distance.

'What's that boat?' I said to old Schultz, who had

come up to see one of his engineers lay out a petty officer in the last fight.

'Ormolu,' said Schultz, adding a few unpleasant words. I had much sympathy with poor old Schultz. The Huns had played every kind of dirty trick on him, and he had done his best to make the old ship go, and now here he was, running round like a kitten after its tail, while the 'Ormolu' looked on.

'Do we get a tow from her?' I asked.

But Schultz became so nasty that I went away.

Until it was dark the 'Ormolu' hung about, and there was a rumour that we would have to get a tow after all, though I do not think this was feasible. No one knew what was really happening except Schultz, who was down in the engine room again, and the Old Man. And the Old Man could look more like a Tasmanian Devil than anyone I've ever seen if he was annoyed. He didn't of course have two rows of teeth, but he showed what he had in a horrid way if he was put out, and had that same whiskery kind of a look. I knew a man down near Queenstown who got bitten by a Tasmanian Devil he was trying to tame and had to have his hand off. He also died of blood poisoning three days subsequently, so they might have left the poor chap alone.

Ordinarily we would have had a lively crowd in the smoke-room after a boxing contest, but no one seemed in very good spirits. All the more sensible officers, such as myself and Jerry and the rest, were not feeling very hopeful. I won't say we had the wind right up, but we all knew that anything might happen before we got to Fremantle. It was now Wednesday, and we were due on Thursday night or early Friday morning, but no one knew how much way we had lost over the breakdown. We would all willingly have got out and swum home if it had been a little nearer.

10

The Padre gives a helping Hand

That evening after dinner some of us were looking over
the rail and smoking. We could see the lights of the
'Ormolu' looking very pretty, a bit ahead of us. It was
clear to all that she must have had instructions to stand
by, or she would have been out of sight long before,
which was not particularly cheering. But it was all pretty
peaceful, and I was just saying something to Jerry to that
effect, when we heard shouts and yells coming from the
first-class cabins. Jerry and I jumped to it, and were down
the companion way in a flash. The noise seemed to be
coming from the far end, forward, and we raced down
the passage. I could see Jerry was feeling for his revolver
which he now always wore, strictly against orders, and I
was glad I hadn't got one, for I don't like firearms, pre-
ferring my fists in a mix-up. Halfway down the passage
we collided with Catchpole who came out of one of the
cross alleys, carrying a kid.

'Hell,' said Jerry, 'they haven't done in a kid, have
they?'

'He's only scared, sir,' said Catchpole, putting the kid
down. It was Major Brown's little boy, a nice kid of six
or seven.

'As far as I can make out, sir,' Catchpole said, 'some of
the troops are fighting down that end in the gentlemen's
bathroom. This young gentleman says he was playing

with his ball, sir, when a lot of soldiers came running past and knocked him down.'

The kid was all right and wanted his ball back.

'All right,' I said, 'I'll find it for you. Take him along to his mother, and pass the word to Mr Howe and Mr Hobson quick and lively, but don't let anyone else know.'

Catchpole went off with young Brown, and Jerry and I ran on towards the bathrooms. There was blood and broken glass about on the floor, so we knew they were at it with bottles. The bathrooms were in another of those cross alleyways. When we got there, the first thing I saw was my big friend Heenan, the one that had tried to knife me at Colombo, with a broken bottle in his hand. He and another big fellow whose face I couldn't see were going for two smaller chaps, and as we came up one of the little fellows went down like a log. I dragged him out by the heels. It was poor old Higgins, with a nice cut across his head.

'Go and meet Howe and Hobson,' I said to Jerry, 'and come round both sides of this alleyway.'

He made off, and I dragged Higgnis out of the way and took off my belt and tunic, because I always find the way tailors cut coats it never allows for free movement, and there are few things more annoying than to feel the arm ripping out of your coat just as you are beginning to enjoy yourself. I also did something of which I am rather ashamed, which was to take my belt. A belt is a weapon I have a great distaste for, but I really don't see how I could have done differently than I did, because those great fellows had bottles, and very likely had knives, and certainly would not have been above kicking below the belt.

I did all this much quicker than it takes to write it, and joined the party. The two big blokes were hammering away at the third, who was putting up a good fight. They hadn't much room to swing their bottles, but they were trying to do a nasty jabbing kind of downward stroke. I caught Heenan such a crack on the hand with the buckle of my belt that he dropped his bottle with a yell, when luckily it smashed to smithereens and was no more use. My belt wasn't much good now at such close quarters, so I chucked it behind me and used my fists. He was a bit heavier than myself, but hadn't much knowledge, and fortunately his pal couldn't get at me in the narrow alleyway, owing to Heenan being between us. However, my foot slipped, and I fell backwards through one of the bathroom doors and the big fellow on the top of me. I hadn't time to be sick, or I would have been. I knew it was pretty serious now, and there was too much noise for me to hear if Jerry had come back. I managed to slam the bathroom door with my foot, and with the two of us on the floor up against it, the other chap couldn't get in. Luckily we rolled over a bit and I got on top of Heenan and gave him a good crack on the jaw.

Then I heard Jerry and the others doing a little peaceful persuasion outside, so I washed my hands and face and came out. They had got the other fellow well in hand, and just as I came out he went right down on the back of his head and passed out. I was very sorry to see it was Cavanagh. The fellow he had been hammering was young Casey, as we discovered when we had wiped his face.

At this moment the lights got very dim and then went out.

'I'll skin Schultz for this,' said Jerry. 'Anyone got a torch?'

Hobson had, so we had a look at the casualties. Heenan and Cavanagh didn't worry me, as they would be dead to the world for some time, but I was worried about Higgins. However he came round a bit presently and he and Casey told us how the row had started. Cavanagh and his cobbers had a plan to raid the crew's quarters, partly for the fun, partly to see if there was anything they could borrow. Higgins and Casey had been asked to join in, but in such a nasty way that they preferred not to. Heenan, who had been well known for making trouble on the Melbourne waterfront, then called them scabs and other names and said they were a couple of officers' narks. The crowd got so nasty that Higgins and Casey took to their heels, but being cornered in the bathrooms put up a good show.

Then Higgins fainted again, so I told Hobson and Howe to get him up quickly to the first-class surgery and pass the word along to Doc Bird. Bird wasn't a very live wire, but he was a white man, and I knew I could rely on him.

Cavanagh and his mate then began to show some signs of coming round, so we stuffed some sponges into their mouths and took them to the door on to the well deck, which was luckily quite close to. Here the lights having gone out proved very useful to us. We could see the door at the end of the passage, because it was a fine night, though no moon, and the door made a kind of light patch, but no one was likely to see us. So we dumped them there, and then I got my tunic and belt. Jerry went into one of the bathrooms to wash his hands, which he had dirtied on Cavanagh, but his luck was out again and the water came boiling hot out of the cold tap, thus causing him to swear.

Hobson and Howe had the torch, so we kept on striking matches till we had got Casey tidied up. He didn't look too bad, and he said he could tell his pals he had run into something with his eye in the dark. I also found the ball the Browns' kid had lost, just by my tunic.

Jerry and I went up to the surgery. It was a bit awkward finding our way in the dark, and we were glad when, halfway up, the lights came on again. There was a great noise of laughing and cheering, and we reckoned the diggers would find enough to amuse them and keep them quiet, chiacking the engineers.

Higgins was our next job. Old Bird had been seeing to him, but he was pretty sick.

'See here, old son,' I said to Jerry, 'this is the Meds' job. You and Howe and Hobson don't know a thing about Higgins. Go and amuse the women; and Jerry, you might tell Celia I'm all right. And give this ball to Mrs Brown's kid.'

Bird was a good old sort. He asked no questions, and when he had done all he could for Higgins he gave me a stiff drink and had a look at my head. There was a bit of a lump, but nothing to speak of. We had a yarn about things and what to do with Higgins. It was a bit of a puzzler. The bad eggs would probably finish him off with knives, or lose him overboard, if he went back to his quarters. I hadn't another orderly I could trust to look after him if he went to hospital, and murder in a hospital is a thing I won't stand for.

'See here, Doc,' I said. 'I'll go and see the missis. If the worst comes to the worst I'll have him in our cabin. Celia can chum up with Mrs Jerry for a night or two. Catchpole won't talk.'

So I went on deck to look for Celia, but the more I thought about it the less I liked it. Catchpole was safe enough, but you know how ships are. Things get about, and the more you don't want them to, the more they do. I knew I was safe for that night, because Cavanagh and Heenan wouldn't be too keen on letting the mob know what a mess they had made of things besides which they would be probably feeling pretty sorry for themselves.

There was a little dance going on aft, and I didn't want to butt in and alarm Celia, so I wandered down forward and sat on a seat under the smoke-room window. There was someone on the seat, and I didn't see till I sat down that it was Father Glennie.

Well, somehow we got yarning, but I couldn't pay proper attention, because I was worrying about Higgins all the time. Time was running on and the question of poor old Higgins not any nearer being solved.

'See here, Padre,' I said, 'is it all square about confession and all that?'

'How exactly?' he said.

'Well, if you are an R.C. and go to confession, can you bank on the padre not doing the dirty on you?'

'That's a very big question, Major Bowen,' he said.

'Big or small, can you keep a secret?' I said.

'The best way to keep secrets is not to tell them,' he said. 'I'm afraid I can't do anything in the confessional line for you, as you aren't one of our people.'

Then he rather hesitated and said in a kind of way as if he weren't quite sure how I'd take it:

'But if you care to think of me as a man, and if I can help you, I give you my word not to split.'

Well, I'd always liked Father Glennie, and now I felt the biggest kind of a skunk not to have trusted him right away.

'Good-oh, Padre,' I said. And I told him about Higgins and Casey and the rest being in a fight and scaring a kid.

'I can take it out of Casey all right,' said Father Glennie, 'and I'll skin Heenan and Cavanagh for this if they come to me, but Higgins isn't one of my lot.'

'It's not a roaring up he needs, Padre,' I said. 'It's just Christian charity. Cavanagh and his lot have half killed him already, and I can't let him go back to their quarters. I feel it's my pigeon, because Higgins is my orderly, and

163

it was trying to keep the others off raiding the crew's
quarters that he got done in.'

Then Father Glennie made me tell him the whole
story again from the begining, to get it clear.

'I see,' he said. 'Well, Major, send Higgins along to my
cabin and I'll keep him for you.'

'But why, Padre?' I said. 'He's not an R.C.'

'Because of what you said,' Father Glennie answered,
'Christian charity.'

I couldn't say anything for a moment. To think of an
R.C. showing me what Christianity really was. It gave
quite a shock to a lot of my ideas.

'Are you afraid I'll convert him?' said the padre.

'You couldn't convert Higgins, Padre,' I said, 'anyway,
not in the state he's in at present. But you don't know
what you're taking on. Some of the biggest scum in the
boat are out for him, and if they find out where he is
they'll knife you, or get you down and kick you, and
think no more of it than breaking a rabbit's neck. You're
too good a man to spare.'

'So is Higgins,' he said. 'If courage and faithfulness
count for anything, Higgins is better than either of us.
As for knives, I haven't been a parish priest in Port
Adelaide for five years for nothing. Can you bring him to
my cabin, or shall I give you a hand?'

'I can manage, Padre,' I said.

'I'll expect you as soon as lights are out, then,' he said,
and off he went.

I just sat and thought a bit. I've known a lot of brave
men in my time, but none braver than Father Glennie.
I've thought differently about R.C.'s ever since.

So I went along and found Celia, and told her I'd have
to be up late with some casualties. She looked rather
worried, but I couldn't explain then.

When I got back to the surgery I found old Bird sitting up reading a novel by Edgar Wallace. Higgins was asleep, but feverish and restless and Bird said he had had a nasty crack. He had sewn up his head all right, but he must have had a bit of concussion as well.

'See here, Doc,' I said, 'we don't want to get the diggers guessing about Higgins. I can't send him back to his quarters, I daren't send him to hospital, but I can make him disappear, and if you don't want to know where, go to bed, and don't look.'

So the old Doc went into his cabin and I sat with Higgins till the lights were put out. Luckily the padre's cabin was on the same side as the surgery, so I didn't have to carry him far. There was only the one berth, but the padre had made a shakedown on the floor for himself. I got Higgins to bed and told Father Glennie what to do, but I found he knew quite a lot about first aid. So I told him to roust me out if anything happened and went off to bed.

If this had happened at any other time there might have been a real bust-up about it, but being so near Fremantle, and the whole boat-load hardly knowing by now whether they were on their heads or their heels, I banked on no one asking too many questions about Higgins for a couple of days. If anyone asked me, I could say he was in hospital, well knowing that they wouldn't trouble to go and look. I may say that when we did get to Fremantle old Doc Bird got him taken off in an ambulance, and we left him there. I heard from him afterwards, and as before stated he is now doing quite well up Goulburn way and has a wife and two kids.

That night I heard the engines moving again in a way that showed me Schultz had patched things up, and when we woke up the sun was on the right side. Routine went on much as usual that day. Cavanagh and his friend never came near the surgery, from which I gathered that they didn't want it to be known that they were casualties. I got word later through young Casey that Cavanagh was very sorry for himself and could hardly see out of his eyes, and Heenan was groaning and being sick all the time. Under any other circumstances I would have gone to see them, but I didn't officially know that they were sick, and I was only too glad that the pair of them couldn't get into mischief for the present. Casey got some Epsom salts from Bird's orderly and said he had given them both a good dose to keep them quiet that night. He never smiled as he said it, but I could see pretty plainly that he knew that the diggers were up to some devilry that night, and wanted me to know that two of the ringleaders would be out of action.

The only other event of a long worrying day was that the diggers held a sale of work in aid of themselves. The work consisted chiefly of anything they had borrowed from their cobbers. It was open for officers from three to four, and to the troops afterwards. Jerry and I went down, and the first thing Jerry saw was some of his war souvenirs the diggers had pinched at Devonport. He fairly hit the roof and wanted to fight the lot of them, but the diggers were very fond of him and they made the fellow that pinched them give them back. Jerry gave him a quid, so there was quite good feeling. After four o'clock all the diggers came to see what of their own property was to be seen, and it was mostly a free fight after that. Some got their own things back and some borrowed some of other people's.

Old Colonel Picking had what he called an officers' meeting that morning, but it might as well have been a mothers' meeting. Andy wasn't there, and as a matter of fact I happen to know he was locked in Colonel Picking's cabin, owing to a threat from the diggers to throw him

166

overboard. This was a decent act of old Picking and made up in some way for his general inefficiency.

We had pretty certain information that the diggers meant to raid the crew's quarters that night, but no way of stopping them. Picking had seen the Old Man, who wouldn't believe him. Stone and Anstruther said they must keep their ratings out of it if possible, but they would join in themselves with the greatest of pleasure. Finally we came to the conclusion that the most we could do was to have good officers on guard at all doors leading from the first-class decks to the men's quarters and hope for the best. Father Glennie had so put the fear of the Church into his lambs that we got several revolvers back, though they were mostly useless, the diggers having considerably damaged the mechanism before returning them, which put the laugh on the padre. But this wasn't really a bad thing. If no one had firearms we were less likely to have serious casualties.

Well, I can't tell you much about that night, for poor old Higgins was pretty bad, and I and Father Glennie were up most of the night with him. I heard a certain amount of noise going on but it was all away from us, and so long as the diggers didn't start killing each other in our quarters again I felt they could go to hell as far as I was concerned. Catchpole had promised to stay up and let me know if anything serious occurred, so that I could go to Celia.

As far as we could make out a party of diggers did raid the crew's quarters, but the crew were ready for them, and after knives and bottles had been freely used the diggers retreated in some confusion. The loss of Cavanagh and Heenan had weakened the morale of the mutinous party and Father Glennie had frightened some of his flock. There was only one attempt to get into our quarters, from the door near the lower deck surgery, but

167

Howe, Stanley and Hobson kept them off with the threat of shooting. If the diggers had been properly drunk they wouldn't have been stopped by a little thing like that, but the beer had come to an end some days before. What was also in our favour was that the electric lights failed again, and no one really wants a free fight in the dark.

About two o'clock in the morning I decided I could safely leave Higgins. I was pretty dead to the world after the crack I'd had on my head the night before, and longing to hit my pillow. Father Glennie looked like a ghost. He was one of those men that just get along with willpower, having very little physique. I daresay he found religion a help too. I left him in charge and went off to bed.

I opened the cabin door very softly, in case Celia was asleep. But she turned on the light by the berth and sat straight up in bed, pointing a revolver at me.

'What's up, kiddie' I said. 'Who gave you a gun? Put it down, and don't shoot your old man.'

Celia took one look at me and dropped the revolver on the ground. I noticed it made no noise. I picked it up, and it was an india-rubber water pistol.

'What's this in aid of?' I said.

'To frighten them, if they came,' said the poor kid, and then she began to howl till I thought she'd never stop. She had got an idea I was down among the diggers and would be knocked on the head and thrown overboard. She had been lying in bed, hearing all the noise and shouting, and had got it into her head the diggers would come to our cabin, and she was going to scare them with a water pistol she had borrowed from young Dick. Can you beat it? Just think of the pluck of that kid lying there imagining heaven knows what, thinking she could stop anyone coming in with a water pistol. I could have kicked myself for not letting her know I was all right, but I had to keep dark about Higgins, and to tell the truth I was so worried about him that I had clean forgotten Celia. Then it all came out how frightened she had been ever since Colombo, and when she saw the 'Ormolu' and thought how we might have been on her, safe and comfortable, it quite got her down. I showed her the bump on my head, which gave her something to think about and cheered her up wonderfully.

There is perhaps something to be said for the R.C. custom of parsons not being married. It would make them worry less about danger and similar things, knowing they have no one at home to be anxious. I would have enjoyed the scrap in the bathroom twice as much if I hadn't remembered Celia and not wished to be carried out stiff. On the other hand it must be quite dispiriting for an R.C. padre, say at the end of a hard day's work, with perhaps several services, and a funeral, and having to deal with drunks and larrikins, not to find his little missis at home with a nice tea all ready for him. But we can't all have everything.

11

Good old Aussie once more

I am now coming near the end of my story. We had had a
rotten deal, but we got some fun out of it too. When we
sighted Fremantle the worst was over, for we were in
touch with Defence then and the diggers couldn't play
up the way they had been doing. It only remains to tell
how we got home.

Next morning Fremantle was actually in sight. It was
late summer, or very early autumn, and there must have
been bush fires up in the hills, for we could smell the gums
right out at sea. More than one of us felt quite sentimental at seeing the good old bush again. It was after twelve,
midday, that we tied up, having made pretty good going
since Schultz got the machinery going. Of course everyone was wild to go ashore, but there was a lot to be done
first. Old Colonel Bird got busy with the medical
authorities, and before anyone left the ship a stretcher
came on board and poor old Higgins was taken away to
hospital. I had carried him to the first-class surgery while
everyone was on deck, hanging over the rail and pointing
out things to each other, and the stretcher-bearers fetched
him from there, so no one knew where he had been for
the last thirty-six hours. His pals were much upset about
it, and they scrounged round and collected his kit,
borrowing anything they needed to make it up, so that he
left the ship with more property than he brought on

board. The digger is wonderfully decent to a sick cobber, and there is nothing he won't do for him.

Presently we heard that there would be twenty-four hours leave for most of us, except for those on duty. Old Doc Bird was very keen to get up to Perth and see his sister, whom he hadn't seen for forty years, so I said I'd stay on board. The Fairchilds were going up to Perth with the kiddies, so Celia was to go along with them and I was to join them at the hotel the next day if I could get away. I was a bit disappointed not to show Celia her first sight of Aussie, but reflecting that I'd have the rest of my life to do it in, I soon recovered. Doc Bird said he daresaid he'd have had enough of his sister by breakfast time, and if so he'd come back and relieve me.

Several of our passengers were leaving us to go home by the Transcontinental, among them Captain Smith, the Browns and their kiddies, and the Peels, the ones that had had the measles. We had no business to let them leave the boat really, but the kiddies had had it so lightly that the spots didn't show, and it seemed a shame to keep them on board, especially as their mother was a real wowser, never happy unless she had a grouse against someone. Besides, if the health officers at Fremantle didn't notice, I felt there was no reason for me to interfere. No use keeping a dog and barking yourself.

I saw Smith before he went, but I don't think he knew a thing about what had happened. Whether he pulled himself straight or not I can't say, as that was the last I saw of him. I never lost any sleep about him.

There was a big mail waiting for us, but only two letters for me. My family had lost interest in me during the War. If the Mater had been alive, she would have written. She was a great little hand at writing letters. I could have wished I had a larger mail when I saw everyone else with stacks of letters, but then I hate writing

171

letters myself, so why blame others? I had a letter from Sis, giving me a lot of news about a crowd of people I'd never heard of, and a cheery letter from little Moses Colquhoun, the one that got his pants peppered at Gaba Tepe. How he had kept track of me, or found out I was on this ship, I don't know. Anyway this was to wish me the best, congratulate me on my marriage and tell me to look him up as soon as I came to Sydney. This I did, and as I told you earlier, he proved himself a real good pal.

The diggers were all ready to take what is called French leave but it wasn't so easy for them here, with quarantine, and sentries from shore at all the gangways. However, finally they got off, and such of us as were left on board were well and truly pleased to be rid of them for a few hours.

Just as it was getting dark, Colonel Picking sent for me. Why he didn't send for Major Barrett I don't know, as he was his second in command, but somehow the Major, though mind you he was a nice old chap, didn't seem to cut any ice and we would have done just as well without him. You may have noticed that I have not mentioned him much. That is because he never did anything. He would come to the meetings and just sit there till they were over. If he hadn't been senior Major he would never have been heard of. What Picking wanted to tell me was that the crew had walked off the ship and said they wouldn't come back till the prisoners had been trans-shipped.

'I don't blame them,' I said.

But all Picking could say was what should we do? I was about fed up with that remark of his, so I said there was an officer in charge of disembarkation at Fremantle and why didn't he ask him. It wasn't a doctor's business anyway. So presently they got hold of Captain Lewis, the officer in charge ashore, and I left them to it. I shall not go into details, especially as I do not know all that occurred, but what happened in the end was that we were held up for three days at Fremantle while telegrams passed between Picking and Lewis on the one hand and Defence at Melbourne on the other, the result being a nice long holiday ashore for most of us. There was also the best free fight I've ever seen between the diggers and the crew. It took place on the wharf, the onlookers joining in according to fancy. The big arc lights were on, and Hobson and I leant over the railing and saw everything comfortably, and the casualties were taken to hospital, so we had no trouble.

Next day Doc Bird turned up bright and early. He said his sister had been like a small belly-ache when she was a kid, and she was a larger one now, and I could take all the leave I liked. So Hobson and I got a taxi and drove up to Perth. In those days it was a taxi, or a slow dirty little train, but now I believe they have motor buses running every half hour.

Well, we had a bonzer time in Perth. The lot of us hired two cars and we went right up into the hills for the day, as far as the big new dam at Mundaring, taking the kids and their nurse. It was great to be out in the bush again. There were a few fires here and there. You'd see some little flames through the trees, looking for all the world like a bush of those azaleas. The air was as clean as creation and the smell of the gums was good-oh. We had lunch at Mundaring and a good sleep on the hot grass, while the kiddies paddled. I must say though that the ring-barked trees all around had not a very pleasing effect. It was the same at Mount Lyell, where looking down south from the entrance to the mine you saw nothing but dead white gums as far as you could see. What they do is they ring-bark the trees which gradually

173

kills them. Then they run a fire through, and after that
the young growth makes splendid food for cattle. But it
always seems a waste of good timber to me, besides
spoiling the natural look of the place.

I had always promised Celia a good drink when we got
ashore, so we had Minchinbury's sparkling hock that
night at the hotel. Coming straight off a dry ship it went
to the kid's head and she made us all laugh. So then we
left Dick and Mary with their nurse, and all wandered
out to one of those little open-air theatres they have in
Perth in the hot weather, and saw quite a good variety
show.

Next day we kept ringing up the ship, but there was
no news of her leaving. At last Doc Bird rang me up to
say we were due to leave at noon next day, so the following morning we all went down early, as I didn't want
to take advantage of the Doc's kindness. He told me the
guard was to be composed entirely of officers till we got
to Melbourne, and we were not to stop at Adelaide
because of possible further trouble there with the crew.
Mrs Jerry was as savage as a meat axe, because she didn't
know whether she would try to make a dash for the
Transcontinental which left the next day, or go on to
Melbourne and take the train back. Finally she decided
to leave the ship, so she raised hell to get permission and
to get her luggage. Somehow she got all her trunks
brought out and packed. I never thought she would have
time, but she said she had lived long enough on the
'Rudolstadt' to know that if it was scheduled to leave at
noon it would be lucky to get away before midnight, and
so it was. There wasn't another woman who could have
got around the baggage master and had all her trunks
got up out of the luggage room, but when Mrs Jerry had
made up her mind you had to get out or get under. We
all said goodbye with many regrets and I gave the kiddies

each an English sovereign that I had managed to get hold of early in the War. We often have the kids over to us in the holidays, and Celia sometimes goes over to the Fairchilds for a trip. I can't get away much at present, but I am taking a partner, and then I'll get a spell from time to time.

I missed Jerry greatly for the rest of the voyage, also Mrs Dicky, who was a nice bright little soul. We had no further troubles except an unpleasant feeling among everyone. The officers had revolvers issued to them at Fremantle, so we had no difficulty in keeping a proper guard going. Old Picking made the officers hold a court-martial on the ringleaders and they pronounced all sorts of sentences, but they knew it was all eyewash. I kept out of it and stuck to the surgery. We had plenty more patent food in, and I spent my time trying to fatten up those poor little kiddies, who certainly did me credit after a week in the Bight. Apart from an appendicitis case which old Doc Bird cut up on the third day out, we had little else to do but weigh the babies and check the stores.

Some hopeful chaps thought there would be an armed guard at Melbourne, and the prisoners would be taken off in irons, but they were expecting a shipping strike, or a train strike or something in Victoria and hadn't any time for us. No, the diggers who lived in Victoria or Tasmania just went ashore quite peacefully or otherwise, and that was all.

The night before we got to Sydney I was down in the lower deck surgery, shutting up shop, when Father Glennie came in with Cavanagh.

'Here's a friend of ours who owes you an apology, Major,' he said.

'That's all right, Padre,' I said, 'I'm big enough to look after myself.'

'See here, Mr Bowen,' said Cavanagh, 'if I'd known

that bastard Higgins was a pal of yours, I wouldn't have stoushed him, see?'

'Right-oh, Cavanagh,' I said, 'and I'm glad I stoushed your pal Heenan, and I only wish I'd hit him a bit harder.'

Cavanagh grinned, and we shook hands and he went away.

'I'm sorry we'll be saying good-bye, P dre,' I said. 'Perhaps we'll meet again. I haven't thanked you decently for looking after poor old Higgins. It makes me feel pretty small, I can tell you.'

'If I did God's work as you do, Major, I'd be a better man,' he said.

This made me feel my name was mud, so I looked out of the window.

'All right, Padre,' I said, 'you're one of the best.'

'I shall pray for you my son,' he said.

Well, I don't know that I wanted to be prayed for, but he was doing the decent thing as he saw it, so I thanked him and said I was sorry I couldn't reciprocate.

'Think of me sometimes when you've been up all night with a patient, or a woman having a kid,' he said, 'and that will do as well.'

We shook hands like old friends and I've never seen or heard of Father Glennie again. If ever he reads this book and remembers the way he kept the sergeant in his cabin, he will know he isn't forgotten.

One last occurrence happened which I must not omit to mention, having said earlier that I would do so. You may remember that Celia had a picture with the medieval name of 'Melencolia' by some Boche artist, which she was wonderfully fond of. Well, the customs weren't bothering the returned diggers, but one of their men who came aboard in Sydney Harbour wanted to

know what the picture was. Celia had it done up care-
fully and carried it in her hand so that the glass wouldn't
get broken, and I suppose he thought it was something
very valuable. Anyway he made a bit of a fuss about it,
and wanted to know what it was worth, and whether she
meant to sell it and so forth, till Celia got a bit fed up,
especially having to untie it and tie it up again. So she
said:

'It's a family portrait, and that's my auntie and her
flying fox that she makes a pet of.'

So he went away quite pleased.

I wanted to call this book 'My Life on the Ocean
Wave', or 'How I nearly didn't survive to write it', but
a friend of mine who is very literary, having several times
contributed to the 'Sydney Bulletin', says that wouldn't
do. So he gave me the title you see on the outside. It may
be literary, but I still think mine is better.

Common Reader Editions

As booksellers since 1986, we have been stocking the pages of our monthly catalogue, A COMMON READER, with "Books for Readers with Imagination." Now as publishers, the same motto guides our work. Simply put, the titles we issue as COMMON READER EDITIONS are volumes of uncommon merit which we have enjoyed, and which we think other imaginative readers will enjoy as well. While our selections are as personal as the act of reading itself, what's common to our enterprise is the sense of shared experience a good book brings to solitary readers. We invite you to sample the wide range of COMMON READER EDITIONS, and welcome your comments.

commonreader.com